freedom city

freedom city

philip becnel

Philip Becnel
2017

First Printing: 2017

ISBN 978-1-387-41604-2

Philip Becnel
Washington, D.C.
www.philipbecnel.com

Contents

Acknowledgements

This novel is an homage to "The Monkey Wrench Gang." Thank you, Mom, for loaning me your Edward Abbey books when I was still too young to understand their brilliance. Rest in peace, Mr. Abbey.

Lien, I love you. Thanks for reading my stuff and tolerating me when all I wanted to talk about was how to build bombs and trebuchets.

To Chris and my fellow writers in the D.C. Public Library writing workshops, thank you for reading my drafts and giving great feedback. Thanks in particular to Cicely, Colin, and Jennifer for very generously donating your time to proofread for me.

I couldn't have written this book without you all, and for that I am eternally grateful. Thank you!

Foreword

Although some of the names and the underlying sentiment of this book are as real as a thrombotic stroke, the facts themselves are purely satire. Several colleagues implored me to change the names in this book, lest I be sued for defamation—but I declined to do so. The reason is that I refuse to believe, despite some recent evidence to the contrary, that the average person is incapable of discerning facts from fiction. This book is fiction. I made it up. If Donald J. Trump, the petulant idiot, or anyone else named herein chooses to sue me, and if a judge or jury agrees that I have defamed that person in any way, I hereby declare that I will blow out my own brains, for I do not wish to live in a world devoid of commonsense.

Prologue: The Aftermath

Despite the odium and widespread condemnation of Donald J. Trump, 45th President of the United States of America, he passed with all the fanfare of a fart in a mesh sack. Medical examiners said it was a thrombotic stroke, likely exacerbated by obesity and high blood pressure. Some said cocaine and opioids had been found in his system, but these reports were never confirmed. Trump was dead, and now it was time to start glossing over his dismal legacy and perpetuating his vision, posthumously, for Making America Great Again.

On the one-year anniversary of his death, Trump's remains were entombed at the National Donald J. Trump Memorial a (mostly) solid gold mausoleum at the Trump National Golf Club Bedminster, in horse-country New Jersey. The Grand Old Party planned an ostentatious ceremony to unveil the impressive tomb, replete with a performance by half the Rockettes and a menagerie of other quasi-famous people who were either unconcerned about their reputations or had no choice but to attend. Besides the expected Republican bigwigs—House Speaker Paul Ryan, Senate Majority Leader Mitch McConnell, many others—the event drew thousands of run-of-the-mill fanatics from around the country.

Special shuttles ran non-stop between Newark and Bedminster all morning. By ten o'clock a sea of red hats—the ubiquitous Nazi armbands of post-Trump America—filled the entire fairway of the first hole. A few Confederate flags were unfurled. Countless signs were displayed. Among them were several varieties espousing the two prevalent conspiracy theories of the lunatic fringe: "Trump Lives!" and "Killary did it! Locker up!"

An intelligent observer, if there was one, might have commented that the event was as much a funeral for English grammar and American exceptionalism as it was for the dead, would-be dictator.

The mausoleum itself, far larger than most of the average spectators' mobile homes, was positioned near the tee box, draped with three football-field's worth of red velvet and gold trim. The jib of a giant crane hung overhead with ropes ready to lift the veil. A stage had been erected beside the tomb. The green was fenced off for the more prestigious attendees, who sat in neat rows of plastic lawn chairs, surrounded by reporters and photographers. Here were the politicos, the CEOs of companies that had profited from the regime, and hundreds of sycophants who had one way or another weaseled their way into a VIP invitation.

Seated among the sycophants, in the very last row, barrel chest concealed by a cheap suit, bald head glistening in the sun, was one Stanley Congdon, the czar of the Alt-Left Terrorism Task Force, or "ALT Task Force," a conglomeration of volunteers and law enforcement officers drawn from different agencies with the goal of stamping out leftwing "terrorist" groups. Sitting beside Stanley—technically *among* the sycophants, but rationally removed from them—was Nick Reddy, one of the Indian architects who had designed the mausoleum. The two men, worlds apart, made polite small talk as the sea of red hats out on the fairway bobbed in unison to a hard rock eulogy performed by Ted Nugent.

When the camouflage-clad rocker finally left the stage, everyone kneeled in self-effacement during thirty minutes of prayers led by President Mike Pence. Tears were shed. A few of the more evangelically inclined lunatics out on the fairway began to speak in tongues.

Miracles duly performed, souls saved (for the moment) from the demonic scourge of liberalism, Ivanka Trump took the stage to kick off the big unveiling. Her speech proclaimed—without a hint of irony—that her father was the greatest President in American history. The crowd on the greenway chanted, "U-S-A! U-S-A! U-S-A..." Everyone on the green, politicians and sycophants alike, Stanley Congdon included, took up the mantra—for to remain silent was to be unpatriotic.

Even Nick Reddy moved his lips, although he didn't say the syllables, for he was not a Christian or an American. Still the jingoism was intoxicating, like Bhakti in Hinduism, only shallower. For just a moment, it made him *wish* he were an American, although that moment passed quickly. In the designer's estimation, there were certainly great things about America, the breathtaking architecture of Louis Sullivan, for example. But it was difficult for him to imagine anything truly creative happening in the United States anymore. His niece Geeta had married and had a son by an American man, but they had moved back to India. Conformist throngs tend to sully things of beauty.

As the voices grew hoarse and the chanting began to wane, Ivanka directed the engineers to lift the veil. Her husband, real estate scion and White House advisor Jared Kushner, joined her on the stage, and with their arms around one another they pivoted to the red velvet drapery.

The bills of the red caps on the fairway turned too. The crowd held its breath. The ropes connected to the crane's main block tightened. The corners of the veil began to creep upward. The red bills lowered, as the crowd hoped to see the first glint of revealed gold. When the sunlight finally hit the shimmering metal base of the mausoleum, the crowd gasped. It was an impressive display of wealth, a tomb fit for a king or an emperor.

Although Nick was seated in the last row on the green, his view was better than those on the fairway, and nobody knew the mausoleum better than he did. The structure was roughly the same size as the Ho Chi Minh Mausoleum in Hanoi, but the base and the columns were made from a steel framework encased in gold that mimicked the grand pillars of a neoclassical design. It was not the mausoleum he had wanted to build, but it was what the Trump family wanted: shiny and imposing.

It was Nick who first realized something was wrong.

Whereas his design of the base had been intended to resemble simple blocks made of gold, as the veil was pealed back he could see that there were now elaborate engravings etched on the "blocks." What was this? He could make out flames, faces, torsos—all incredibly intricate—but he was too far back to see what they were. Without thinking, he shoved his way through the throng of sycophants, straining to make sense of the etchings. He could see squiggly lines, wings, more faces, a turtle, words, a briefcase—a swastika?

Up on the stage, Ivanka's hand went to her mouth. Jared continued to smile, oblivious. Some members of the crowd lifted their caps and began to scratch their heads. The boom swung behind the mausoleum, taking the red velvet covering out of sight. There was some clapping far back on the fairway, but everybody close enough to see the tomb was momentarily stunned into silence.

On the green, the politicos in the front row gawked at the tomb in horror. They were the closest, and they could see plainly their own faces etched into the gold. The workmanship was flawless, breathtaking. The photographers scrambled for the best shot, clicking picture after picture, zooming in on the details of the amazing collage.

In the chaos that ensued, Nick found that he was standing in the front row directly beside President Mike Pence, who stared, lipless-ly, soullessly, at his own likeness. On the base of the mausoleum, directly in the center, Pence's effigy chewed on a severed dick while standing atop a mountain of many more severed dicks. It was both grotesque and brilliant.

Stanley Congdon had followed Nick to the front and now stood on the other side of President Pence. "Holy shit..." he said, drawing a glare from the President.

To Nick, a student of art, the etchings resembled the great Renaissance painting, "The Fall of the Rebel Angels," by Flemish master Pieter Bruegel the Elder. It clearly depicted a clash of two great forces, with angels on the four columns fighting back an army of "demons" gathered at the base. He noticed the exact likeness of Ivanka Trump, a halo atop her head, smiling into a mirror in which she was reflected as a hideous ghoul with bleeding boils on her face. Senator McConnell, depicted as a turtle, had eaten most of his own body and was now only a head and a bloody shell. Each image that caught Nick's eye was more striking than the last one.

There were six angels, one on each column, all diverse and heroic. Each resembled a playing card: an ace, a king, a queen, and a jack on the inside columns, flanked by two jokers on the outside columns. The queen, with a beret à la Patty Hearst, appeared to be scaling her column as a monster clutched her boot; only the creature's hand was beginning to crumble where it touched her. Another angel, the jack, wearing a cowboy hat, had cracked a swastika in two and was using it to bludgeon the beasts below him. The ace, with pointy hair like a joker's hat, appeared to be carving bombs into the pillar. The bombs rolled downward as he carved, exploding into the monsters' bodies. The king was bearded and wore a modern suit. Above his image was a halo, and he was surrounded by an aura that seemed to singe the demons below. The two jokers were women, one wearing a Native American headdress and the other a real Indian, draped in a saree and with a Bindi on her forehead. The Indian woman looked familiar—but it couldn't be. Nick shook his head.

"How could this happen?" the President asked Stanley Congdon through clenched teeth.

Mesmerized by the vandal's incredible workmanship, Nick responded to the question without thinking: "The artist used aqua regia. It's an acid used to etch gold. Incredible…"

"The *artist?*" Pence scowled and turned his back on the designer, again addressing the czar of the ALT Task Force. "How close are you to catching these terrorists?"

"We're close, Mr. President," Stanley said. "We know who they are, and we think we know what they're planning next."

"If you know who they are, why haven't you arrested them already?"

"I didn't say I knew *where* they are—yet."

Pence nodded and glanced around to make sure there were no reporters within earshot. "Well, what they are planning next?"

Stanley stared across the President's shoulder at Nick for a moment, decided the designer was probably harmless, and said: "They're planning an attack on the White House."

"The White House?" Pence laughed. "What makes them think they can get their little ragtag gang into the White House?"

"I don't know, Mr. President, but that's what we think they're going to do next."

Pence pointed to the desecrated mausoleum. "Find the people who did this, Mr. Congdon. That's an order. They'll fry for this."

President Pence then turned and stormed off the green, flanked by Secret Service agents, swarmed by reporters. Stanley Congdon went looking for the Secret Service director so he could insert himself as the head of the investigation.

Nick turned back to the mausoleum and admired the intricate workmanship. Whoever did the etchings was a phenomenal artist. Nick had never seen anything like it before. It was every bit as impressive as Michelangelo's masterpiece at the Sistine Chapel, but it had been done with *acid*. It actually looked like the etchings were meant to be there, like they were part of his design. Moreover, the artist must have done all this work in less than two days, which was when the tomb was veiled.

Secret Service officers began cordoning off the area and pushing reporters off the green. Nick flashed his credentials, but he was told to leave anyway.

"This is a crime scene now," an officer said.

Nick nodded and then stole one last look at the collage etched on Trump's tomb. It was a thing of beauty—there was no other way to describe it—probably the most masterful work of political sabotage the world had ever seen.

"Maybe my niece's husband was right," the designer said to himself. "Perhaps there is some hope left in America, as long as there is someone still here willing to fight for it."

1. Origins I: Beach Sands

"This may be the best martini I've ever had." Beach Sands, Esq., forty-eight, son of former-hippies, beard brushed with gray, cheeks pink from gin, raised his glass to the beautiful bartender, whose nametag identified her as "Grace D." Based on her accent, he guessed she was from the Philippines. A foreigner working for an anti-immigrant demagogue: it figured.

"Thank you, sir."

"You don't have to—" No, it was better she didn't know his name. He took another sip. Salt and juniper berries: proof of Dionysus' existence. "Nobody goes out of their way to be honest anymore."

"I try to be honest." She reached up to return the bottle of pricy gin to its perch on an upper shelf. Her skirt climbed up her pantyhose and clung high up on her slender hamstrings. Her uniform and the wall of bottles behind the counter were likely designed for just that effect.

"Everyone *tries* to be honest, but nobody goes out of their way anymore."

The bartender turned, un-clung her skirt, and began busying herself at the sink.

Beach emptied half his glass. "Sometimes we lie because we don't say something that needs to be said. For example, I hate this fucking place, but the three martinis you've made were excellent. It would have been dishonest had I left without acknowledging it."

"Thank you?"

"There are other times when something is so obviously wrong that not speaking up about it is a lie."

"What brings you to Trump International Hotel?" she asked.

"Biological warfare."

She laughed. "Now *you're* being dishonest, sir."

"Am I?" Beach finished his drink. "I'll tell you what, let's play a game."

"I'm working. I can't play games."

Beach swiveled toward the lobby behind him. Magnificent crystal chandeliers dangled from white-painted trusses, which zigzagged across the massive room. All of the sofas and dining tables were empty. Besides a housekeeper pushing a cart stacked with clean linens along an exterior corridor a hundred feet above the trusses, they were the only ones there. He turned back to the bar. "You get to ask me a question—any question—and then I get to ask you a question, and we both have to answer honestly."

"Like truth or dare?"

"Right, but without the dare part."

She opened her mouth and then closed it. Her eyes dropped to his tie, on which he had already dribbled some of his martini.

Beach's gray suit was at one time the nicest he owned, reserved for the opening arguments of his felony trials, but that was ten years ago. Now one of the sleeves was missing a button and the lapels were a bit too wide. A bulge in his jacket pocket made the whole suit seem ill fitting. In the bartender's eyes he would have seemed comparatively mediocre sitting next to her regular customers: Saudi royalty and Russian oligarchs.

"Why are you *really* here?" she asked.

Beach finished his glass and rested the stem gingerly on the bar. "I admit biological warfare is only one reason I'm here." He glanced at his watch—3:58 p.m.—and he pointed to one of the hotel rooms beyond the trusses. "My girlfriend is up there right now fucking someone she met on Craigslist."

Her mouth opened. This time it stayed open. "Really?"

"Really. Now it's my turn to ask you a question."

"But you didn't tell me—"

"We never agreed on giving any explanations beyond the bare truth." He rested two hundred-dollar bills on the counter. "How do you feel about working here, knowing what these people stand for?"

She took the bills from the counter and walked to the cash register, where she pressed some buttons, waited for the receipts to print, placed those and Beach's change in a book, and set the book on the bar in front of him. "I don't care about politics," she said. "I have a two-year-old son."

"An honest answer," Beach replied, sliding the book back to her without opening it.

Like clockwork, Clare Swan, his twenty-seven-year-old-legal-assistant and friend-with-benefits, emerged from an elevator and glided across the lobby as smoothly as if she were riding a Segway.

Her gray pencil skirt was twisted slightly askew, and her chestnut hair, before arranged in a neat ponytail, was now free and gently tussled. But these were details only Beach would have noticed. He grinned appreciatively. Clare smirked and walked to the bar, sitting down beside him.

"Welcome to Trump—" Grace D. began.

Clare held up her palm. "I'm good, thank you."

"How was it?" Beach put a hand on her knee and began sliding it up her skirt. He couldn't help himself. She smelled like sex. It made him crazy.

With thumb and forefinger, Clare removed Beach's hand from her thigh as if it was a glove found on the sidewalk. She then turned it over and placed in its palm a plastic card: the room key and elevator fob she had swiped from her date. She glanced at the bartender, who was again busying herself at the sink. "The… meeting went well. Are you ready?"

"Yes."

"I'll meet you outside."

Beach watched Clare sashay to the exit. She was built like a thirteen-year-old boy, which is how he liked his women: no hips, flat chest, knobby knees, and an underdeveloped frontal lobe. He was a lucky man. He stuck the fob in his pants pocket and turned back to the bartender.

"That's your girlfriend?" she asked.

"It's complicated. Thanks for the drinks, Grace D. You've been swell."

Beach stumbled into the restroom, where he lightened his gin-sodden bladder on the floor directly beside the toilet and wrestled a paper lunch-bag containing a Mason jar from his coat pocket. On the nights when he had drunk too much gin—which was most nights—he was fond of proclaiming to anyone within earshot, "The only thing worse than a bedbug is a hypocrite." Sometimes Beach replaced the word "hypocrite" with other objects of his disdain: "racists," "fascists," "religious nuts," "Mike Pence apologists," and sometimes "Phillies fans."

When he was still married to Sarah, their house had been twice infested with bedbugs. It was a nightmare of 1980's Hollywood slasher-film proportions. It started when they began discovering welts on their extremities, which they first rationalized must be mosquito bites (Talk about being dishonest with yourself). It was only when they saw splotches of black blood on the sheets that they figured out what was happening: a full-blown bedbug infestation. They had to pay an exterminator named Willy thousands of dollars to get rid of the evil little things. It took weeks, and it was the final straw ending in his divorce.

Willy told them bedbugs mate through traumatic insemination. The male literally pierces the female's body with its penis and injects its sperm into her abdominal cavity. A more evil creature Beach couldn't imagine, except...

"The only thing worse than a bedbug is a fascist enabler," he said to himself as he peaked into the bag and turned the jar around in the light. Thousands of bedbugs climbed along the inside of the jar, looking for a way out—looking for a way to eat flesh, shit out black blood, and ruin lives.

Bag in hand, he left the restroom, hung a right toward the elevator lobby, and swiped the fob that afforded him access all the way up to the penthouse level. This was no easy task. Security at the Trump International Hotel was tight, even with Trump dead now for three months. But Clare's Craigslist date, Garth Simonson, was a project manager for a security outfit called Backwater Mercenaries. Garth lived in Fairfax, Virginia, just an hour away. Staying in the penthouse suite, even though he really had no need to be there, not only gave him an excuse to be away from home and cheat on his wife; it would also help his company get Department of Defense contracts. Booking the overpriced rooms was the easiest way to bribe the regime. Welcome to post-Trump America.

On the hotel's top floor, Beach carefully unscrewed the Mason jar, leaving the mouth just below the lip of the bag. He then strolled the corridor and casually shook out five or six bedbugs near the door of each room. When he was done with the top floor, he rested the cap back on the jar, accidently squishing two of the critters (Nobody promised there would be no casualties). He brushed off two or three that had escaped onto the carpet. He then took the elevator one floor down, where he repeated what he had done on the penthouse level.

When he traveled down three floors and had shaken the last of the bugs out of the jar, he rested it and the paper bag, still open, in the trash receptacle of a cleaning cart. It would be a month before the hotel was completely infested. In the hotel business, news of a massive bedbug infestation was bound to cost them a fortune in treatments and lost bribes. Willy had only charged Beach five hundred dollars to collect the bugs, and it had only taken him three weeks.

Three blocks away, Clare was straddling her bicycle, absentmindedly staring at her phone. She had put her hair back in a ponytail and was now wearing a bike helmet. "How did it go?" she asked.

"They won't know what hit them."

He moved to kiss her, but she held out her hand. "Not until you change clothes and take a shower. Let's go to the other hotel."

"Then you'll tell me what you did up in the room?"

"He was good with his hands."

Beach snorted. She went back to looking at her phone while he yanked off his tie and tossed it in a trashcan. He did the same with his coat and trousers, until he was standing on the street in dress shoes and socks, a pair of day-glow orange boxers, and a once-white t-shirt that was now dyed bachelor-pink. Realizing he had thrown away his wallet and keys, he reached into the trashcan, fished out his trousers, returned them to the receptacle, and fumbled with his bike lock. The hotel where they would clean up and rehash the day's adventure was near Dupont Circle, less than a mile away. There were clean clothes waiting for him there.

"Do you love me?" he asked as he climbed on his bike.

"No."

"Liar."

She looked up at him again for the first time in five minutes and burst out laughing. "Are you riding to the hotel like that?"

"Fuck the world."

She tossed her phone in her bag and shot up 15th Street like a lithe, hipster rocket. He pedaled hard to catch up. She was more than twenty years younger than him and at least fifty pounds lighter, and she was also athletic. She rode her bike everywhere, didn't own a car, didn't eat meat, did yoga, swam, and eschewed sweets. Beach did none of that. He could feel what was left of the gin sloshing around in his belly. He was no match for her.

Thankfully, she caught a red light on Connecticut Avenue, allowing him to pull up next to her, panting heavily. "What else was he good at?"

"You have to wait." She shot into the intersection, despite the red light, weaved past several slow-moving cars, and disappeared into the congestion of Dupont Circle.

2. Origins II: Langston "FD" Hamdi

Gazing out the window of the W3 bus to Anacostia Station, Langston Hamdi, affectionately known as "FD" (pronounced "Ef-dee"), twenty-five, artist, skin like polished walnut, dreadlocks like an aloe plant—a stoic, bright, hulking young man—brooded over his mission of revenge. When his brooding began to feel too much like hatred, FD pulled a permanent marker from his bag and began to draw on the back of the seat in front of him.

The hatred was always there, like the whiff of urine in certain alleys. But nothing in the world—not Nana, not music, not alcohol, not weed, not Prophesy, not Anijah, not D'Andrea, not Darrisha, not even Solette—nothing eviscerated, at least temporarily, the ever-present undercurrent of hatred more than the simple, selfless act of beautifying his environment. Starting at the bottom, he drew a canister that resembled a bullet and then a long, sloping "S," ending midway up the seat.

"If art doesn't make us better, then what on earth is it for?" his father often said, quoting poet Alice Walker.

No man had had as big an influence on FD as Bilal Hamdi: father, husband, musician, philosopher, troublemaker, and hustler—now two years deceased—a victim of lung cancer caused by his long-time day job: abatement worker. His father's death had upended FD's world, causing him to drop out of Howard University, where he majored in Engineering. It had been Bilal who had given Langston his nickname, which stood for "Full Deck"—as in, "That boy there's playing with a *full deck* of cards."

This was in contrast with many others in the Woodland Terrace public housing complex who had been dealt something less than a full deck. Many of the boys FD grew up with were now dead or in prison. Most of the girls his age already had kids old enough to refer to him as "Uncle Ef-dee." The smarter ones had moved to Maryland a long time ago. But FD, like his father before him, stayed put—a monk with a Metro card and some talent whose feet brushed poverty, addiction, oppression, and violence, but whose legs and torso somehow managed to walk above the pitiless water that drowned everyone around him.

Many disaffected young men, and some women, scribbled on various surfaces with a Sharpie Magnum, but FD preferred a more refined marker, the Sharpie Chisel, which had a much narrower tip and gave his art more detail. With practiced skill, he sketched out the familiar face: prominent lips, nose, balding dome, careless beard, and downward sloping eyes. He had to stop there. Drawing his father's eyes always brought FD to the verge of tears. To him, those eyes were the embodiment of love, and like drawing anything ethereal, it was difficult to make them look as perfect as he could see them in his mind.

The W3's path took FD west, down Morris Road, zigzagging over to Martin Luther King Jr. Avenue and the heart of Anacostia. His phone rang—the same unfamiliar 703-number: a Virginia number. He refused the call and switched off his phone completely. He had heard of people getting caught doing stuff because their phones tried to log into wireless networks near the scene of the crime and ended up leaving a trail.

Gentrification had not touched Anacostia as it had the parts of D.C. west of the Anacostia River, though speculators had long drooled over the area's obvious potential. The bus passed an overweight mother pushing a stroller and talking on her flip-phone. She wore glittery flip-flops and a tube top, her stomach jutting out on all sides. A group of older men congregated outside a barbershop were laughing at something. One was holding his sides. A young couple whispered to each other near a wall, on which was spray-painted the self-righteous, repugnant face of President Mike Pence. Above it was the declaration, "Fuck Racism." The mural was FD's work, and around it were his people.

But he was heading east today, out of the city. With a few lines he connected the sloping "S" of the oxygen tube to his father's nose and used a fingertip to strategically smear some of the ink around the eyes to give them depth. He then stowed his marker, slung his backpack over his shoulder, swiped his Metro card, and was soon underground heading to Branch Avenue Station. From there he would take the Route 30 bus to Clinton Fringe, in Prince George's County, Maryland, where lived one Officer John G. Meyer of the Metropolitan Police Department (MPD).

Ironically, Officer Meyer was at that moment on patrol near FD's home, which was three blocks from the MPD's Seventh District

Station. Therefore, Officer Meyer wouldn't be home again until sometime after 6 a.m. the following morning, when his shift ended. FD had made sure of this.

It had been a month earlier when Officer Meyer and his squad of jump-outs—adrenaline pumping, guns drawn—had stormed into the courtyard behind FD's apartment, where he lived with his eighty-year-old Nana. Like every night of the week that FD could remember, the courtyard was filled with people, some smoking weed, all talking and joking. And like on many nights, the police barged in on the party, barking orders, frisking people, shining flashlights in the corners. FD had been through this a thousand times. He watched the scene from the safety of his backdoor stoop, a joint in one hand, an iPhone filming the spectacle in the other. His unflinching attitude and the fact that he was documenting the scene clearly irritated Officer Meyer, who marched over to FD, red-faced, yanked him out of the doorway, and unceremoniously threw him to the ground. Rifling through FD's pockets, Officer Meyer found three ounces of weed inside a Ziploc bag.

FD was arrested for possession with the intent to distribute. Possession of up to two ounces of marijuana was legal in D.C., provided it was only smoked on private property. FD had been in his doorstep, which *was* private property—but Officer Meyer had claimed on the arrest paperwork that the weed was plainly visible in the courtyard, a public area, at the time of the stop. Worse, as the arrest had happened so quickly, FD had been unable to lock his phone, and the video he took had mysteriously disappeared. The lawyer he retained, some hotshot recommended by the *real* neighborhood drug dealers, assured FD the case had a good chance of being dismissed at the next motions hearing, since they had gotten an "alright" judge. But that still left the matter of repaying Officer Meyer for his flagrant violation of FD's civil rights. Nothing stokes hatred quite like having one's nose rubbed in the urine-imbued humiliation of injustice.

At the Clinton Fringe stop, he walked south for a quarter mile on Branch Avenue and took a dirt path that led through a patch of woods on the outskirts of Officer Meyer's neighborhood. FD knew the way because he had previously been there to retrieve his phone from the undercarriage of Officer Meyer's shit-brown Chevy Cavalier ("Find My iPhone": the poor man's GPS tracker). The neighborhood was mixed, working class, and rural. There were cars on blocks and dogs on chains, and many of the yards were strewn with plastic swimming pools, trampolines, and children's bikes. Meyer lived alone—or at least it appeared he did. His lawn was unkempt, more dirt than grass, no toys, no dog shit; the blinds were dusty; and there was no second vehicle.

FD knew that as a young black man he would draw attention walking alone, and so he walked with purpose, his chest jutting out with the confidence of someone who belongs there. He imagined his father in a hardcore band, pounding on his bass guitar in front of a mostly-white audience of teenage punk rockers. *He belonged there; I belong here.* It was late enough that there was nobody on the street. A dog barked at him from a window. FD ignored it. He followed the streets to Officer Meyer's blue clapboard rambler, strode across the yard, and glanced at the neighbors' houses just long enough to ascertain that nobody was outside. He then kicked open the front door with a single blow from his size 13 boot.

Inside, he closed the door and stood still. His heart was beating Bad Brains-fast. That was what had inspired his father as a kid to become something different: seeing the Bad Brains—before there was even a thing called "hardcore" music—perform in the courtyard at Woodland Terrace. FD was not even born when the Bad Brains came, but his father had told him the story a thousand times, how the whole project stared at the band like they were crazy—which they were. However, that night Bilal Hamdi decided to break from the mold, scream at injustice, and make his own music.

FD listened for any noise that might indicate he had drawn attention to himself. In the silence of the night, the explosion of the door bursting open had seemed deafening, but he knew it would quickly be forgotten, provided nobody had seen him. After two minutes, hearing nothing inside or outside of the house, he decided it was safe to get to work, but he waited longer still, to let his eyes adjust to the darkness. He donned his gloves, opened the dingy blinds to let in the moonlight, and went about searching the house.

Officer Meyer's laptop was beside his bed. It was a P.C. This was convenient because FD could remove the hard drive and bypass the password, whereas most Macs are encrypted. He slipped the laptop into his backpack. In a kitchen utility drawer he found a thumb drive and an old phone. The battery was dead on the phone, so he couldn't tell if it was locked or not. He tossed it and its charger in his bag. He looked in the freezer, where he found a police-issued body-worn camera, a bottle of Jack Daniels, and an envelope containing eight hundred dollars in cash. He stuffed the cash in his pocket, poured the whiskey down the sink, and put the camera in his bag. He returned the empty bottle and envelope to the freezer.

A thorough search of the house turned up two more thumb drives, a digital camera, a massive collection of pornographic DVDs—mostly of the girl-on-girl variety—and a chrome .357-magnum revolver. FD kept the electronics and the pistol, and as an afterthought swished Officer Meyer's toothbrush in the toilet before replacing it on its holder. He then looked out the window to make sure none of the neighbors were out on their porches. When he was confident the coast was clear, he stepped out the front door, closed it as best he could behind him—the wood of the doorjamb was split in two—and used an alcohol wipe to clean his boot print from the door. He then walked casually back to Branch Avenue. He had fifteen minutes to catch the last Route 30 bus back to the Branch Avenue Station.

FD couldn't wait to see Officer Meyer again at the motions hearing in a couple days. He would have no idea it was FD who'd broken into his house. Perhaps, FD thought, there might even be something on the electronic devices that could help his attorney get the case thrown out.

An hour and thirty minutes later, the W3 dropped him off on Langston Place in Woodland Terrace. Although the street was named for the poet Langston Hughes, it had been for this street that FD was named, not by his father but by his mother. It was where FD's grandfather, his father's father, during the 1970's, had changed their family surname from Washington to Hamdi. The family had not remained Muslim past his grandparents' generation. FD walked up Ainger Place, passing a fourteen-year-old lookout named Junior, who was perched in his wheelchair.

"Sup, Uncle Ef-dee?"

"You got a DVD player?"

Junior nodded. FD handed him one of Officer Meyer's DVD's: "Squirting Stories, Vol. 9."

"Shit, thanks!"

"Don't tell anyone where you got it."

FD heard the party before he turned into the courtyard. A thumping bass, laughter, a hundred people congregated, young and old, the smell of weed, past a pit-bull on a chain, kids feeding it pieces of a biscuit, hood-rats jockeying for his attention, several obligatory gangsta hugs: this was home.

He slipped into his Nana's house, closed his bedroom door, and dumped the contents of the backpack onto his mattress. The gun bounced to the floor. He hid it in the same hole in the wall where he kept his bankbook and then began removing the hard drive from Officer Meyer's laptop. FD knew about computers from working at Best Buy, and he had a collection of SATA drives for just this purpose. He screwed the hard drive into the SATA and plugged it into his own laptop. Within twenty minutes he found a Word document with a list of passwords, plus Officer Meyer's Outlook backup and web history.

FD switched his phone back on. It was almost 3:30 a.m. He had two more voicemails from the same 703-number. But he only had three hours before Officer Meyer would arrive home, discover the break-in, and start changing his passwords. FD had a long night ahead of him. He put in his ear buds, turned up the volume, and got to work.

3. Origins III: Joseph Kaline

It had taken Joseph Kaline ten years to reinvent himself, from an angry, impulsive, shit-stomping, young redneck with delusions of fighting in an imaginary race war, to an unflappably liberal, semi-respectable private investigator working criminal defense cases in one of America's great, diverse cities: Washington, D.C. Raised in a shotgun house in a blue-collar, alcoholic family outside San Antonio, Joe was whipped nearly to death by his father, a construction foreman; spent his teens in residential treatment facilities, courtesy of social services; and then spent the first couple years of his adulthood roaming the south with various skinhead crews, until a fight outside of Atlanta landed him in jail. There he was beaten repeatedly and raped with a broomstick, but the worst trauma had been to his identity, when the kindness of an African American inmate nicknamed "Rock" made the attacks stop and for the first time in Joe's life he realized what an ignorant, homicidal asshole he had become, just like his father.

The morning after FD relieved Officer Meyer of his cash, pistol, and electronic equipment, Joe—now with hair like an orangutan, broad of shoulders, resolutely repentant—pulled his blue Toyota Corolla onto Langston Place and wrote on his legal pad, "Hamdi – 9:32 a.m."

Mr. Langston Hamdi had retained Beach Sands, Esq., who in turn hired Joe to take some photographs of the courtyard and the doorway where Mr. Hamdi was standing when he was arrested. Joe was also supposed to ask Mr. Hamdi about any witnesses who could testify they saw Officer Meyer yank him out of his apartment into the public space of the courtyard. The only problem was that Joe had tried calling Mr. Hamdi a dozen times, and Mr. Hamdi had not returned his calls.

Joe slipped his legal pad into his briefcase, slung the bag over his shoulder, and walked to Mr. Hamdi's front door. There, he knocked. When there was no answer for over a minute, he knocked again. The curtains of the only window parted, and a round, kind, elderly, bespectacled face blinked at him through the glass.

"Yes?" said the woman.

"I'm here to see Langston Hamdi. I work for his attorney."

"I'll see if he's here." The face disappeared. There was talking inside. Soon the face reappeared. "He's not home. Do you have a card?"

Joe reached in his jacket and dug out a card, which bore his name, title, phone number, email address, and his D.C. private detective license number. He wedged the card between the door and the doorjamb. "Please have him call me. Also, I need to take some pictures of your backdoor."

"If I had a nickel every time a boy asked me that…"

"You're funny."

Dirty-minded old ladies: if there was clearer evidence that the world was fundamentally okay, Joe couldn't think of it.

He walked around the building and entered the courtyard from Ainger Place. It was empty except for a teenage boy in shorts and a wheelchair feeding a flock of pigeons. Joe greeted the boy and watched the winged rats scamper for breadcrumbs. Although the kid was older than Joe's son, his bare, atrophied legs reminded Joe of Naagesh's legs: innocent, spindly, the color of café au lait.

When Joe was released from jail, he used what money he had to purchase some backpacking equipment, picked up the Appalachian Trail at Chattahoochee National Forest, and hiked it all the way to Maine. Along the way he singed off his skinhead tattoos with a red-hot frying pan. In Maine he saw snow for the first time—didn't like that one bit—and hiked south again to the Blue Ridge Mountains. He intended to continue southward to warmer parts, perhaps to reconnect with his sister back in San Antonio, but along an overlook on Skyline Drive he chanced to meet a rock-climber named Geeta, a stunning, slender, George Mason undergrad from India. It was Geeta who led Joe off his self-loathing purgatory on the mountain and onto the path of a new beginning.

That hopeful path, as it turned out, had been short. Five years later, Donald J. Trump, the personification of all the hatred Joe had rejected, was elected President of the United States, and shortly thereafter Geeta had been forced to return to India. Although Naagesh was a citizen, Joe let her take their son, then two years old, home with her. He would be better off in India, raised by Geeta's family. Post-Trump America was no place to raise brown kids.

"You a fag?" said the wheelchair-bound boy. "Why you staring at me?

Joe shook his head. "I work for Langston Hamdi's attorney. Did you see him get arrested a few weeks ago?"

"Naws. I don't know no 'Langston Hamdi.'"

The boy tossed the rest of the crumbs to the pigeons and pushed himself to one of the apartments. There was a small ramp. He rapped on the door, it opened, and he wheeled himself inside.

Joe was now alone with the pigeons. He retraced his steps to Ainger Place and counted the doors until he identified the Hamdi home's backdoor. He snapped a picture. He then took some wider shots of the entire courtyard before returning to the backdoor again for some close-ups.

In his camera's viewfinder he was startled to see someone looking back at him from the window. It was not the wrinkled, bespectacled face of the foul-mouthed old woman, but the long, square-jawed, masculine face of a twenty-something African American man with dreadlocks jutting out in all directions, not unlike an aloe plant. Joe lowered the camera, but the man was gone. The curtains swayed.

"Motherfucker," Joe said under his breath.

He took out his phone and pressed the button to redial Mr. Hamdi's number. He could hear the phone ring once inside the apartment, and then the ringing stopped and on his phone he heard, again, the familiar greeting.

"Hi, this is Carl Kasell of National Public Radio's 'Wait Wait... Don't Tell Me!' Ef-dee made me do this." Here the unmistakably white, baritone radio announcer cleared his throat and did his best Tupac Shakur impersonation. "'Thug for life, beyatch! Yeah, nigga, thug life, from now until for mother-fuckin' forever. Have-nots in this, motherfucker—' Please leave a message!"

Beep!

"You can avoid me if you want, Mr. Hamdi, but you're the one paying me."

Joe hung up, snapped a couple more pictures, stowed his camera back in the bag, and returned to his car. His card was gone from Mr. Hamdi's front door.

Joe had three other stops to make before he returned to his home, which was in Arlington, just across the Potomac River, in Virginia.

There he would do some online research and write reports until it was time to eat dinner, have his weekly Skype chat with Geeta, jerk off, and go to bed. Joe was a simple man.

He had been a private investigator for two years, and Mr. Hamdi's case was his first for Beach Sands. After following Geeta to Northern Virginia, he applied to George Mason University too. As a former ward of the State of Texas, his tuition was fully paid for. He majored in Cultural Studies with a minor in English. Shortly before he and Geeta graduated, a classmate happened to go on a blind date with a private investigator named Phillip Nichols. The classmate and Phillip hadn't hit it off, but she started working cases for him during her senior year. When she graduated and got a "real" job, Phillip needed someone else to work her cases, so Joe jumped on the opportunity. It turned out that he loved being an investigator. Every day was different, and the people he met were in turns squalid, resplendently flawed, and (in his assessment of humanity) perfect. But his favorite part was that for every person he helped to keep out of jail he was giving something back for all the years he spent espousing ignorant bullshit. He believed strongly that everyone—well, almost everyone—deserved a second chance.

His next stop was on Chesapeake Street, Southeast, just on the D.C. side of the border along Southern Avenue. From Woodland Terrace, he turned right on Alabama Avenue and stopped at a light in front of the MPD's Seventh District Station. Out front a pugnacious white cop was standing next to an illegally parked, shit-brown Chevy Cavalier, waving his arms hysterically at a group of other officers. They looked at Joe. He gave them the finger. The light turned green. He continued down Alabama and had only traveled a block when his phone chirped: an email.

The secret to being a successful private investigator, as taught to Joe by veteran investigator Phillip Nichols, was very simple: keep your phone alerts on and respond to attorneys immediately.

"Attorneys are the most unreasonable bitches on the planet," Phillip said on Joe's first day, "but when it comes right down to it they don't know shit about what investigators do and they're happy enough if you just respond to their emails quickly."

Joe glanced at the phone, one eye still on the road. The email subject was "Officer John G. Meyer, Metropolitan Police

Department." Joe didn't recognize the email address. At the next light he read the message.

"Dear Private Detective Joseph Kaline, The attached link contains evidence that the arresting officer for one of your impending cases is a perjurer and a racist." It was signed, "Malcolm X" and contained a postscript: "Thank you for your diligence."

There was a link to a file-sharing site. Once past Suitland Parkway, Joe pulled over and downloaded the zipped file. In it there was a massive MP4 file, a video. He would need his computer to view that. But he was able to view some of the other files from the cockpit of his Corolla. There were pictures, clearly still-shots of the video, showing several cops beating up a boy in the courtyard of Woodland Terrace. Joe didn't know what Officer Meyer looked like, but the boy looked familiar. He looked like the boy he had met earlier, the one in the wheelchair. Only in the video the kid was standing up. Other files included a complaint from a civil lawsuit, pages of a deposition transcript, and a membership card for a group called "Cops for Comeup-Pence."

The membership card alone was enough for Joe to condemn Officer Meyer forever. The group was a known fascist law enforcement club, where racist cops got together and did circle jerks to the regime. Mike Pence was a fucking Nazi, and nobody was surer of this than Joe Kaline—since he had been one too. He had the scars to prove it: one on his upper right arm and another on the back of his left shoulder. Shit, that had hurt. He had bled from Nantahala National Forest all the way through the Great Smokey Mountains. Now the scars of his old skinhead tattoos only burned when he was angry, and nothing made him angrier than willful, unabashed ignorance.

He decided to head home early. His other cases could wait a day. There was something special about Langston Hamdi—Joe could feel it—not in his scars but in his damaged, earnest heart. He was going to bust this case open, and in the deal he would take one step closer to redemption.

4. Origins IV: Clare Swan

"You have plans later?" Beach Sands hovered nearby with the hopefulness of a hopeless, charming dork. He had recently taken to matting his beard down with a greasy balm, and today he wore a cloak that looked like something from a Harry Potter movie.

"I had planned on getting gang-banged tonight by the Washington Redskins." Sitting on the couch in her office—which doubled as Beach's reception area—Clare Swan took a drag on her vape pen: the Dank Fung Executive. It was a bit ostentatious for her liking, what with its 24-karat gold plating, but it had been a birthday gift from Beach, so she used it in his office to make him happy.

"Please, they're the Washington *Football Team*. We don't use racial slurs, not in my office."

"I forgot. I'm almost done with the Hamdi motion."

"Well, as much as I approve of watching you get passed around like a football, we'll have to reschedule such activities until tomorrow. Tonight we have a mission of the utmost importance. We're going to take the fight straight to corporate America. We're going to hit them right where it hurts most. For this we need clear heads. The cocks of football players would only get in the way."

"Cocks always get in the way."

"Cocks *point* the way, my dear." He retreated into his office, waving his papers. "Gang-bangs, tomorrow. Tonight: revenge!"

Of the gifts bestowed upon Clare Swan—whiteness; rich, doting parents; a top-notch education; waifish beauty; a pleasant laugh; empathy; among countless other gifts—none was quite as advantageous as her uncanny ability to see right through the lies people tell themselves to their honest-to-God motivations.

Case in point: Beach was a cuckold. Why was he a cuckold? Because he was desperately scared of being abandoned. The fetish enabled him to control his fear. To Clare, it was the same as women with rape fantasies: they didn't want to *actually* be raped, but by coopting their fear and making it something sexy, they could live with it. She intuitively understood that the more Beach encouraged her to fuck other men the more he was scared of losing her. She played along, not because she loved him—although she might—but because they were indeed sexually, subversively, and existentially compatible in a way she had not encountered in any previous relationship. They were a match made in anarchy.

She had been working on Langston Hamdi's supplemental motion since they received the investigator's report, and it was due to be e-filed in thirty minutes, but the last hit of weed made her mind wander a bit and she needed a break. She stashed the vape pen in its fur-lined box on the end table and glanced at the news app on her iPhone. Mike Pence's lipless face smiled out at her. Now, *there* was an interesting study in psychological profiling, she thought. Somebody so fanatically anti-gay must be harboring some deep-rooted fears. There is no doubt: Pence guzzles cum in his dreams. The article was about federal funding for the National Donald J. Trump Memorial, which was being built at the Trump family's private golf course in New Jersey. She shuddered and shut off the screen.

She tucked her legs beneath her butt and willed her eyes to scroll down Mr. Hamdi's motion one last time. Two weeks ago they had filed a motion in limine that asked the judge to exclude from trial the drug evidence on the grounds that Officer Meyer's search occurred on the curtilage of Mr. Hamdi's property and without probable cause, thereby violating Mr. Hamdi's Fourth Amendment rights. However, they didn't know then that the arresting officer, who had testified at Mr. Hamdi's preliminary hearing, was a proven perjurer. They were now asking for another opportunity to question him before trial. It was a simple motion, which is why Clare was writing it. Judge Wanda J. Swift was a reasonable woman. She should rule in their favor in letting them call the officer again, provided she didn't probe too deeply into how their investigator, Joseph Kaline, got the new information.

When Clare and Beach had met with Mr. Hamdi in his cell before his arraignment, the towering black man with the pointy hair had sat still, ropey arms crossed, hardly saying a word. He didn't smile. He didn't ogle Clare. He barely looked at her. He just listened as Beach explained the process, how he would go before the judge, probably be released on personal recognizance, and how there would be a motions hearing, where Beach hoped they could get the case thrown out. When Beach was done with this standard spiel, Mr. Hamdi had simply nodded and said, "Alright."

As he didn't seem overly concerned about his freedom, she found herself wondering what motivated Mr. Hamdi. The fact that she had no idea was slightly unnerving.

Clare had not planned to work in criminal law, and she had certainly not gone to law school to become a legal assistant. After she graduated from the Washington College of Law at American University, ready to embark on a career in environmental policy, she got arrested for punching a Nazi during a counter protest at a Trump rally. Regrettably, it had not been a solid punch; she hurt her wrist more than the man's face. Scared to ask her parents for help, she accepted the attorney who the court appointed her, one Beach Sands, Esq. He got her case dismissed, and when the arrest held up her application to the D.C. Bar, he also gave her a job.

She sent the motion, making sure to copy Cynthia Truitt, the Assistant U.S. Attorney who represented the government against Langston Hamdi. Quite coincidentally, Cynthia had been the prosecutor on Clare's assault case too. That Cynthia had only graduated law school two years before Clare was likely a factor in her willingness to dismiss the case. Cynthia magnanimously concluded that Clare's actions had been "out of character" for a young, white, female, law school graduate. She had not actually used the word "white," but it was fairly clear that Cynthia saw something of herself in Clare and had decided to cut her some slack. Clare hoped she would cut Langston Hamdi some slack too.

"Come on, Clare. Justice is calling." Beach shut off the lights and strolled out of the office. He had removed the cloak and now had a messenger bag slung over his shoulder.

"Justice? I thought you said our mission tonight was revenge?"

"Same thing."

She followed Beach into the hallway and watched him lock the door. His cheeks were flush. She laughed.

He put his hands on her shoulders and kissed her lips. "Do we have to ride tonight? There are so many places. We could take a Lyft."

She met his gaze. "If you want to hang with me—no unnecessary carbon emissions. Biking is good for you."

"Fine, but can we get a drink first?"

"No." She brushed his hands away and walked down the stairs.

"Can I at least see your tits? I need inspiration."

"No!"

She unlocked her bike first and shot up 7th Street toward Chinatown. Beach's office was near D.C. Superior Courthouse, or "Super Court" as he called it. He only rode his bike to work on the mornings after she slept over at his house, which was in Logan Circle, fewer than two miles from his office. He was such a baby: an endearing, eccentric, man-child. He was sullen when she left him behind at a light in Chinatown, but when she was approaching L Street and looked back to check on him, he was sweating profusely and his face bore the same juvenile grin he flashed on the occasions when she *did* show him her tits. The grin made his lower lip jut out, and it made his eyes crinkly in a creepy-older-man kind of way. But it was hard not to fall for the flattery that she was the object of such unabashed affection.

"Sexy Safeway!" he called after her. "Did you know that back in the day, before all you fucking millennials came to the city, the Safeways in D.C. all had their own nicknames?"

She slowed down to let him catch up. She had heard this all before. Like all men, he repeated himself ad nauseam. Her father did it too. Although he was a tenured professor of mathematics at the University of Vermont, his real passion was history. The man could wax for hours about the Civil War and he loved Greek legends, relaying the various stories of the Odyssey from memory. Clare had been captivated by her father's stories when she was little, but by the time she got to high school she had her own interests: social justice, ecology, law, revolution. Although she appreciated history, it was a piano that could play any tune, depending on the whims of the pianist. Religion was like that too. Given a choice between trusting a history lesson or trusting her instincts, Clare would choose her instincts every time.

Breathing heavily, Beach was droning on behind her. "There was the 'Soviet Safeway' on Corcoran Street, 'Spanish Safeway' on Columbia Road, 'Stinky Safeway' on Georgia—although that one's been totally renovated now and is therefore no longer stinky. Oh, and of course the 'UnSafeway' in Southeast. I had a robbery case there once…"

The Sexy Safeway was the closest to downtown. Once there, they locked up their bikes and traipsed right to the beer isle, which was empty except for a twenty-something white couple staring at the row of wine bottles, apparently waiting for divine inspiration.

Beach stood beside the woman. "Buy the Yellowtail. You won't know the difference anyway."

The couple smiled at him politely, plucked a bottle from the shelf, and scurried away. Clare set to work on the cases of Yuengling, pulling them off their refrigerated shelves individually and setting them on the floor. Beach pulled a stack of three-by-five labels from his bag, and together they began sticking them to the side of each case. The labels read:

Thank you for supporting Yuengling! A portion of the proceeds from your purchase will be donated to President Mike Pence's 2020 re-election campaign. At Yuengling we are committed to supporting American fascism and all it entails, from decimating our natural environment to euthanizing blacks, homosexuals, and other undesirables. Together we can Make America Great Again!

Last week, when Beach had discussed his idea for the labels and had read his draft aloud to her, Clare thought the part about euthanizing was a tad bombastic, but Beach insisted, "It's *mostly* true!" Their owner, Richard Yuengling Jr., famously supported and raised money for Donald Trump in 2016, so the company deserved it. The problem was that people who were otherwise progressive still drank the beer out of habit, so Beach's idea was to educate the consumer through retail-level sabotage. They had similar labels for Coors and Blue Moon, since their Chairman, Pete Coors, endorsed and hosted fundraisers for Trump. Next week they would target Under Armor clothing, whose CEO had endorsed Trump and sat on his manufacturing advisory board.

When Beach had finished with the Yuenglings, he helped Clare stack the cases of labeled Coors back on their shelves. Although they received a few curious glances, nobody said anything to them. When they were done at the Sexy Safeway, they got back on their bikes and rode several blocks to the Giant Food behind O Street Market on 7th Street. Beach beckoned her to follow him around the market and into the parking lot, rather than going straight to the bike racks in front of the store. He stopped at the far end of the lot and she pulled beside him. They gazed across at the supermarket.

Beach reached into his bag and produced two bottles of Yuengling. "To my knowledge, the Giants in D.C. never acquired nicknames." He handed her one of the bottles.

"You don't have a problem with drinking fascist beer?"

"Beer is beer. I didn't pay for it."

She shrugged, popped the cap off with her lighter, and took a swig. "It's not bad."

He downed half his bottle. "It's American swill."

"You're an American."

"I'm a *post*-American." He finished his beer in one gulp. "America doesn't know it's dead yet."

"We should get back to it." She gave him the rest of her beer. She was still high, and she preferred weed to alcohol. "You have to be in court tomorrow."

He guzzled her beer and then launched both bottles across the parking lot. They shattered on the asphalt fifty feet away. "I hereby dub this supermarket the 'Defiant Giant!'"

Clare's anger came so suddenly she found her fists were clenched. She stared at Beach in horror. "What the fuck is wrong with you?"

"It's just glass."

"You're an ass."

Before he could respond, she shot across the parking lot toward the store, careful to avoid the broken glass. She locked her bike before he caught up with her. Once inside the newly dubbed Defiant Giant, they worked in silence. She fumed in anger the entire time. She thought of every time she had punctured a tire because some asshole had broken a bottle on the street. Why did men have to be so childish? When they left the store he tried to hold her hand, but she pulled away. She unlocked her bike.

"Next up, Stinky Safeway."

She pushed her bike onto his legs. "You know, Beach, I'm going to take a Lyft after all."

"But what about the carbon emissions?"

"Fuck you." She stormed across the parking lot toward 7th Street. While Beach trailed behind her, awkwardly pushing her bike, she typed in her address and hailed a Lyft.

"What am I going to do with your bike if I'm riding *my* bike?"

"Push them both."

"Where are you going?"

At the sidewalk she wheeled around on him. "I'm with you on resisting fascism—but you can't break things unnecessarily and trash a place when you're with me. Unlike you, I actually *care* about the world. I don't want to see everything destroyed. I'm not going to stand for that shit."

He swallowed. "I'm sorry."

"Too late. You can do the Stinky Safeway by yourself. I'm going home, and I'll meet you at court tomorrow."

"Please, Clare—"

"Don't forget my bike."

The Lyft pulled up and she climbed in. Beach stood on the sidewalk, still holding her bike. His eyes were glossy. His mouth was open. He looked pathetic, and for a moment, despite her anger, she considered getting out of the car. Instead she lifted her shirt and pressed her tits to the window.

"Is that your husband?"

She turned her head and saw that the driver was smiling at her with all the ambiguousness of a dick pic. She laughed and lowered her shirt. "It's complicated." She couldn't see his face in the shadow, but he had broad shoulders and straight teeth. She flashed Beach a mischievous smile and turned back to the driver.

"Hi, my name's Clare."

5. Super Court Conspiracy

Throughout the hearing, Beach Sands was in turns furious, jubilant, and horny, as he jogged the courtroom like Stephen Curry, landing three-pointer after three-pointer, masterfully confronting Officer John Meyer with the abundant evidence of his shitty character.

Beach's fury started when he watched the video his investigator received from the mysterious "Malcolm X." It was footage from a police body-worn camera showing six cops chasing and then beating the shit out of a thirteen-year-old boy named Junior Smalls. Junior was paralyzed from the incident, and his family subsequently filed a lawsuit against the MPD. The deposition transcript was Officer Meyer's testimony—under oath—when he denied witnessing any of his colleagues assault Junior or otherwise do anything improper during the arrest.

If there was anything worse than a bedbug, in Beach's estimation, it was a perjuring cop.

But if the injustice of the police assault and the cover-up stoked his rage, Beach quite enjoyed questioning Officer Meyer, who squirmed on the witness stand, blond hair in a buzz-cut, teeth clenched, forehead glistening, trying his best to defend his veracity. But the cop might as well have been shouting, "Fake news!" to someone with a college degree.

Meanwhile, Clare's perfume sweetened the air in the defense table's vicinity. They had made up this morning, when she had hinted at her tryst the night before. Now, even amidst all the drama of the proceeding, he couldn't help but steal glances at her knees poking out from beneath her skirt. He imagined them wrapped around the Lyft driver as he fucked her in the back seat. The thought made him crazy.

"Objection!" Cynthia Truitt jumped from her seat for the fourteenth time. The prosecutor wore red-rimmed eyeglasses, which did no more to mask her profound unhip-ness than her pinstripe slacks could make her hips—which were as wide as America—appear slimmer. "Relevance, Your Honor? You may or may not like Mike Pence, but millions of people voted for him and he remains the

President of the United States. Mr. Sands seems to be suggesting that supporting the President makes a witness impeachable."

"If I may, that is *precisely* what I'm suggesting." Beach pointed a finger at the American flag behind the Judge's bench. Just to the right of the flag, displayed on a flat-screen monitor, was a copy of Office John G. Meyer's "Cops for Comeup-Pence" membership card. "This administration, starting from the top, has consistently aligned itself with white supremacists. The fact that Officer Meyer is a bona fide member of Mike Pence's police fan club is absolutely relevant to my motion. It relates to the witness's character and to his bias against my client, who has a Muslim surname and who, as you can see"—Beach gestured to the defense table—"is an African American."

At the defense table, seated beside Clare, Langston Hamdi doodled absentmindedly on a legal pad. He had somehow squeezed himself into a suit apparently tailored for someone half his size, and his massive head, hands, and his pointy hair seemed like they were trying to escape the unreasonable constraint imposed on them. Beach glanced at the doodle and saw that it was a portrait of him, in the courtroom-sketch style, pointing at the flag. It looked exactly like him; the man had serious talent.

Judge Wanda J. Swift—shrewd, one lazy eye, a single gray streak in her hair like Lily Munster's—turned her good eye to Ms. Truitt. "Trump *did* refer to white supremacists as 'fine people.' Doesn't membership in a group that aligns itself with those values say something about the witness's character?"

"But where does it stop, Your Honor? Might simply *voting* for an objectionable candidate be impeachable too?"

"Yes," Beach said. "If you voted for a Nazi, you're a—"

The Judge held up her hand. "I've heard enough. I will allow the introduction of the membership card, and I will take the prosecution's objection under advisement. Now, unless you have more questions for Officer Meyer concerning other issues, I would like to give Ms. Truitt a chance to rehabilitate her witness."

Ms. Truitt shuffled some papers atop the prosecution's table. "I have no further questions, Your Honor."

Beach stepped aside to let Officer Meyer slither off the witness stand. He then turned and addressed the bench. "I have one more witness, Judge. I would like to call Junior Smalls to the stand."

"Your honor." Ms. Truitt's removed her red-rimmed glasses and set them on the table. "The government would like to, um, withdraw its charges against Mr. Hamdi."

"With prejudice, I presume?" Judge Swift said. "No pun intended." The prosecutor nodded. "Very well. Then, this case is dismissed with prejudice, and the court is now in recess." She rapped her gavel on the bench.

"All rise!" called the bailiff.

When Judge Swift left the courtroom, followed by her clerks, Beach pumped his fist and stuck out his hand to the defendant, who was putting the finishing touches on his sketch. "Congratulations, Mr. Hamdi. Your case is dismissed, for good."

"Call me Ef-dee." FD stood and shook his hand. "Thank you, Mr. Sands. Your words were… inspiring."

"Beach." He bent over the drawing for a better look. In it, he was both scowling and smirking, and one of his eyebrows was raised. "That's super! You've managed to encapsulate my trifold personality perfectly. How much you want for it?"

FD slid the notepad across the table. "It's yours."

As they convened in the aisle, there was more friendly banter and back patting. Beach praised Clare for her work on the supplemental motion. He thanked Joe Kaline for his stellar investigation. Joe and Clare complimented Beach for his oratory skills. FD apologized to Joe for not answering his phone calls. Ms. Truitt passed by and complimented Clare's suit jacket as if they were old chums. Ms. Truitt's pinstriped butt then disappeared beyond the swinging doors, leaving Beach, FD, Joe, and Clare alone in the empty courtroom.

Beach put his arms around Joe and FD, leading them to the vestibule. Both men were tall, with sturdy shoulders. "Today we have set an important new legal precedent: we got a judge to agree that supporting Pence makes a witness *de facto* impeachable. Drinks are on me!"

Clare rolled her eyes. "It's not even noon. And the judge didn't outright agree with your argument."

"She let in the membership card, which was as good as acknowledging that anyone who voted for Trump is a Nazi. We'll get the transcript."

She laughed. "That's what *you* said."

Beach released the men's shoulders, swept through the doors into the hallway, and past the squat, angry personage of Officer Meyer, who stepped directly into Joe's path. Beach was shoved aside.

"You're Joseph Kaline, right?" Officer Meyer spat. "I know it was *you* who broke into my house, because I remember you flipping me off yesterday morning on Alabama Avenue. That's how you knew about 'Cops for Comeup-Pence.'"

Joe puffed out his chest and clenched his fists. His face turned the same color as his red mane. "I don't know anything about a break-in at your house. Maybe you should build a wall around it!"

Officer Meyer seized a fistful of Joe's tie and dress shirt and reared his other fist back as if he were about to punch Joe's lights out. Beach grabbed the cop's arm and held it back.

Clare stood on her tiptoes and wedged herself between the men, chin jutted out, staring defiantly at Officer Meyer's face. Joe's head, veined, purple, looked like it might explode with rage.

"There-there, Officer Meyer." Beach tried, unsuccessfully, to make his voice sound soothing and not condescending. "Nobody on my defense team broke into your house. As I said in court, the evidence was sent to us anonymously."

"By 'Malcolm X,' sure…" Officer Meyer released Joe's collar and wheeled around on Beach, yanking his arm free. "Did you know your investigator's got a criminal record? I *saw* him that morning, counselor. He emptied my bank accounts. I know he did it and I'm going to prove it—I can promise you." At that, Officer Meyer turned and stormed down the hallway.

Joe yanked off his tie and paced the hallway like a caged animal, muttering curses under his breath. "Motherfucking cocksucker, I should've knocked his fucking teeth out…"

"What an asshole." Clare picked up a button from the ground that had been ripped from Joe's shirt. "I wonder why he's so sure it was Joe and not Ef-dee?"

"That racist motherfucker doesn't think a 'nigger' could be smart enough to do him like that," FD said. He touched Joe's shoulder. "Man, don't let that sack of shit get to you."

Together they descended the escalators in silence. Joe silently fumed. FD smirked. Clare looked at her phone. Beach hoped they wouldn't run into Officer Meyer again before leaving the courthouse, as he was unsure they could hold Joe back a second time. Thankfully, they made it out of the courthouse and walked the two blocks to Beach's office without another incident.

His reception area contained a desk with no receptionist, a bookshelf of law books, and a pleather couch, with room for three. The couch normally served as Clare's work area. Joe collapsed in the middle, flanked by Clare and FD. Beach went into his office to make drinks. When he emerged, wearing his Harry Potter cloak and carrying a tray with four martinis, the others were laughing and passing Clare's vape pen around. Clare had kicked off her shoes. Joe and FD had removed their jackets and dress shirts and were now both wearing white t-shirts.

"So, what does Ef-dee stand for?" Clare leaned over Joe to pass FD the pen.

"Fuck Drama."

"What I want to know," Joe said, "is how you got Carl Kasell's voice on your phone?"

"My Dad signed me up for 'Wait Wait… Don't Tell Me!'"

Clare laughed. "You're full of surprises."

"To Malcolm X!" Beach said, unfurling his cloak and presenting the tray with exaggerated fanfare. They took their drinks, clinked glasses, and drank deeply.

Clare raised her glass again. "To thrombotic strokes!"

"Hear, hear!"

Joe took another drink. "Is it illegal to wish that Pence drops dead too?"

Beach sat atop the reception desk, his feet dangling over the side like a kid sitting in a grownup chair. He took a moment to look at Clare and their new friends. This was Joe's first case with him, so Beach didn't know him at all. Perhaps boldly, Joe had his arm propped on the couch behind Clare, who was sitting sideways with her legs tucked beneath her butt. Clare, however, was looking past Joe at FD, who looked like he had been summoned from a Calvin Klein advertisement. FD was looking at Beach with a smirk on his face. Of course, they had no idea of his relationship with Clare, but Beach thought the possibilities were interesting.

"As of right now," Beach said, "wishing is still protected by the First Amendment, but there is an amendment in the House seeking to ban all forms of wishing."

"You mean praying?" Joe asked.

"Same thing."

Clare set down her drink and reloaded the pen. "What I don't understand is that when Trump died I thought this country was supposed to return to some semblance of normalcy, but then we have groups like 'Cops for Comeup-Pence,' beating up black kids—and nobody does anything about it."

"What if *we* did something about it?" Joe said.

Beach downed the rest of his drink and arched his eyebrows. "What do you have in mind, Joe?"

"Man, I just met you guys," FD said. "Wishing may not be illegal—yet—but I'm pretty sure conspiracy against the government's a crime."

"Who said anything about conspiracy?" Beach held out his palms. "To be convicted of any crime there must be *mens rea*—a guilty mind or a willful plot—and an *actus reus*: you must actually carry through with it, or try to. What we're doing here, now, is clearly still within the bounds of protected wishing. And I say this as your lawyer—which means it's also covered by privilege."

The vape pen made another round. Even Beach took a hit, although weed tended to make him a tad paranoid. The talk meandered to less conspiratorial topics: the absurdity of religion dictating morality, the tragedy of American fascism, art, music. He returned to his office, made more drinks, and came back with another tray of martinis. Joe's arm was now draped around Clare's shoulder.

Beach returned to his perch atop the desk. "So Joe, what would you do, wishfully speaking, if you had the resources to do something?"

Joe removed his arm from Clare's shoulder and leaned forward. "There are targets all around us. Of course, you've got well-protected government targets, like the White House and the Capitol buildings. Those would be very hard to attack. But there are also thousands of corporations and banks that are in cahoots with the regime. There are fascist propaganda centers like Fox 'News.' You also got the fucking memorial they're building for Trump in Jersey. I'd *love* to do something to that. But if you wanted to start on a smaller scale, just to make a statement, there are literally *thousands* of Confederate monuments all over the South right now. The possibilities are almost endless."

"What would you do to a Confederate monument?" FD asked.

"I don't know. Blow the fucking thing up."

Clare touched Joe's arm and handed him the pipe. "Do you know how to do that? Make a bomb? Wishfully speaking, of course."

"Sure, I could make a bomb."

Beach shot from the desk, stood at attention in the center of the room, unfurled his cloak, and raised his glass to the ceiling. "To revolution!"

"He means *wishful* revolution," Clare said.

"Whatever."

6. The Rubicon

It was with a mind lubricated by gin, animated with weed, besotted by kindred humans, that FD Hamdi, the stalwart monk of Woodland Terrace, broke one of the two vows he swore he would never break: "Only commit felonies alone."

It was this particular vow, unspoken, hardwired in every synapse of his brain, which had kept him out of major trouble, notwithstanding his recent arrest, for the past twenty-five years. But a neurotransmitter somewhere had gone haywire, and now he found himself on a Saturday, sober, conspiring with three white lunatics in a private detective's garage—in Virginia, of all places—building pipe bombs.

It had all happened so fast. The morning after hatching their "wishful" conspiracy, Beach withdrew thousands of dollars from his personal retirement account to fund what he called, "Civil War, Part Deux." Joe made them lists of things to buy with Beach's cash. FD found them all fake IDs and a "borrowed," gunmetal-gray Honda Odyssey from one of his "nephews" in Woodland Terrace—no questions asked. Clare and Joe bought encrypted radios, backpacking supplies, and a handheld plasma cutter, among other sundries.

As he rubbed fertilizer onto a board, grinding it into a fine flour, as the others prattled on about Joe's gun collection, FD wondered whether he could trust his new friends. Why was he taking such an enormous risk? As he often did when faced with a course of action he was unsure about, he wondered whether his judgment was clouded by anger, guilt, or pussy.

Certainly FD's ever-festering hatred had been inflamed at his arrest. But he had avenged himself by breaking into Officer Meyer's home and (hopefully) hurting the cop's career. Also, the trial had vindicated him completely. Was he still angry? Always. But he didn't think it was affecting his judgment, normally so sound.

There was an admitted pang of guilt—somewhere on FD's left side, between his fifth and sixth ribs—that it had been Joe who incurred Officer Meyer's wrath for the break-in. Here was a private detective, quite obviously deranged, who was just doing his job, flipped off a cop (as you do), and now he was a felony suspect. FD genuinely liked Joe, whose Texas drawl and red mane hid a revolutionary zeal as feverish as a Zapatista's. But all revolutions are inherently internal. Whatever demons Joe harbored were not FD's concern, guilt or no guilt. No, it was something else.

He glanced at Clare, who sat across from him at a workbench twisting pieces of cotton twine into a mixture of gunpowder and glue to make fuses. He was absolutely certain he could fuck her if he wanted to—but did he want to? Incidentally, his second solemn vow was to never confuse pussy for love.

A skinny, rich, self-doubting, white girl: Nana would say of Clare, "She's the type of girl who eats once and shits twice."

FD liked Clare's personality well enough, and there was a part of him who wanted to spend a couple hours with her alone, but only in the sense of a check on a bucket list. Like Joe, like all of them, she hid some demons inside too, and getting involved with her would likely be more trouble than it was worth. No, let her indulge her big-black-cock fantasy with someone else.

So, if it was not anger, guilt, or pussy, why was FD there?

More importantly, what would his father think about what he was doing? His father would probably tell him to go paint something beautiful and not stick his neck out for other people. But then, his father died before Donald Trump was elected President, before the fascists became emboldened. Now, keeping a low profile was for cowards—and Bilal Hamdi was no coward. If he were alive, maybe he would be here making bombs too.

FD took a break to watch Joe show Beach how to put the fertilizer he had ground into several shallow pans and cover it with methyl alcohol.

Joe held up another shallow pan and set it in the sink. "Next we'll pour off the liquid from *those* pans into this pan. The dry ice will form crystals of ammonium nitrate that will be pure enough to detonate with a blasting cap."

"And then we'll have crossed the Rubicon..." Beach sniffed the methyl alcohol and shook his head violently.

Clare looked up from her fuse-making station. "Easy, Caesar. That's not gin."

"There's a lot more to do before we have bombs." Joe picked up one of the shallow pans and gently swooshed around the liquid at the bottom. "We need to mix one part motor oil and one part gasoline into sixteen parts purified ammonium nitrate crystals. Then we need to make blasting caps."

Beach noticed FD watching him and smiled broadly. "I feel an ethical obligation to warn you, Ef-dee, that we have herewith crossed the threshold from 'protected wishing' to a full-fledged conspiracy. We've got all the elements of a crime to get us locked up forever: *mens rea, actus reus,* onomatopoeia—"

"Bang!" Joe said, holding up a pipefitting.

Clare laughed. "Meow!"

"As your attorney, I must advise you against participating any further in this conspiracy. If you withdraw now and turn us all in, you'll have an affirmative defense."

FD stared into Beach's face with an artist's eyes. Beach's mouth was creased in a heartfelt smile, lower lip protruding, pink nose, beard barely contained, crinkly, smiling eyes—a troublemaker's eyes, a philosopher's eyes. A neurotransmitter in FD's brain flipped like a switch and revealed the theretofore-mysterious cognition, the actual reason he was there: Beach reminded him of his father.

He leaned back and rubbed his hands together. They were caked with fertilizer and smelled like shit. Everyone watched him expectantly. "No, we cool. I want to blow shit up too." He turned to Joe. "Dude, where'd you learn how to do all this shit?"

"I picked it up here and there."

"It's true," Beach said. "In Texas, bomb making is taught in middle school. Gun ownership is obligatory."

FD shrugged. He didn't fully buy Joe's answer, but he figured a man's past was his own business. Joe certainly knew how to make bombs. He had a lot of guns too, including stuff FD had only seen in movies, like an AR-15 and an Uzi. FD went back to rubbing the fertilizer on the board, while Joe checked out Clare's fuses.

"These are really good," he said.

"I suppose smoking is out of the question?" she asked.

"Absolutely." Joe grabbed two beakers from a cabinet. "Now we need to fulminate the mercury. That's the dangerous part. We'll gently heat five grams of mercury to fifty-five grams nitric acid, and then add that to fifty grams of ethyl alcohol. Mix that with potassium chlorate"—Joe tapped on a bottle sitting on the counter—"and we've got a primary explosive that will set off the ammonium nitrate."

"Then we can get high?" Clare said.

"Then we can get drunk?" Beach said.

"Then we can blow shit up?" FD said.

"Absolutely."

7. Fearless Vampire Killers

It took Joe Kaline a full decade to purge himself of his bigoted stink, but it only took him a week to revert to his former violent tendencies; albeit, they were now appropriately directed. He would never again be racist, but his heart remained full of shame and rage.

Many years ago, during a four-month "survivalist" training camp for white supremacists in rural Arkansas, he had learned how to make a few different types of explosives, detonators, silencers, and incendiaries; how to survive in the wilderness; how to convert semi-automatic weapons to full-auto; and altogether how to foment hatred and terror on Jews and "mud people." Whenever he thought of the things he used to say and believe back in those days, his entire body shuddered with self-loathing.

Meanwhile, his old tattoos burned red hot since his altercation with Officer Meyer. He despised post-Trump America and its deplorable adherents to his soul's core. When Beach proposed waging a guerilla war on the South—where Joe had once been an enemy soldier—he knew it was his destiny.

Or, as Geeta would say, it was dharma.

At the wheel of FD's borrowed minivan, Joe drove the gang south, past the asphalt sprawl of Northern Virginia, past strip malls and a million homes with the exact same shade of vinyl siding: tan. The vehicles got larger, more American. Olive Gardens became Cracker Barrels, which eventually became diners named after female octogenarians. The people grew fatter, less stylish. Soon there were zero pedestrians—no people who were not driving in their massive cars, checking their mail, or cutting their grass atop riding lawnmowers. Farms, gun racks, "fresh eggs," the omnipresent Golden Arches, dead deer, dilapidated buildings; they descended into the belly of the beast.

They stopped to hide two caches of supplies: one at Chester Gap and another near Tinker Mountain, a few miles from Roanoke. One of the things Joe had learned about insurgencies was that it was best to travel light and not to keep anything incriminating with you that you do not need for the operation at hand. They would hide two other caches in similar locations as they made their way further south. His plan was to keep everything near the Appalachian Trail, so that they could escape—all the way to Canada, if necessary—without ever having to show their faces in a major town.

It was midnight by the time they arrived in Lynchburg, the site of Liberty University, founded by evangelical nut-wing Reverend Jerry Falwell. The University was now a breeding ground for extremists of the Christian-Taliban variety, and the perfect place for the gang to test out one of their new pipe bombs.

It took only ten minutes of driving through a residential neighborhood before Clare spotted what they were looking for: a primer-gray, Ford pickup truck with its tailgate covered in rightwing bumper stickers. It was parked in the driveway of a brown rancher with a neatly trimmed lawn and an American flag hanging by the front door.

In the passenger seat, Beach squinted to read one of the stickers. "Infidel Inside."

"Hillary Clinton for Prison." FD, who was seated behind Beach, shook his head in bewilderment.

Joe glided past the home and pulled the van beside a vacant lot a few blocks away. He killed the motor and headlights, then turned to address the others.

"Remember, the key to us not getting caught and going to prison forever is teamwork—and these." He removed four radios from a bag and handed one to each of them. "If we look out for each other, the risk of us getting caught is very low. This target here is gonna be a piece of cake, because we can see the entire block from where we're parked, but when we start on some of the more public targets we might need to post lookouts in multiple places. Got it?"

They nodded, put in the earpieces, and tested the radios.

"Who wants to go first?" Joe held up one of their bombs.

It was a length of pipe about a foot long with threaded caps on both ends. A piece of their homemade fuse stuck out of a hole drilled in one end.

"I'll go first." With gloved hand, Clare took the bomb from Joe.

"Remember, don't bend the fuse—and don't touch the thing with your bare hands. It'll take about three minutes for the fuse to set off the igniter, so that's plenty of time to walk—don't run—back to us. Got it?"

"Got it. Wish me luck." She pulled a skullcap over her head, tucked her ponytail inside, and started opening the door.

"Wait!" Beach said. "I feel like at this stage in the conspiracy our group needs a name."

Clare sighed. "Beach likes to name things."

"Revolutionaries without a name are just anarchists."

"What's wrong with that?" FD asked.

Joe scratched his head. "How about Antifa? Or the Black Bloc?"

Clare fidgeted impatiently with the door lever. "How about White Rose, after the Nazi resistance?"

Beach shook his head. "I think those names are already taken."

"How 'bout the Fearless Vampire Killers?" FD said.

"Oh, I like that!" Before anyone else could object, Clare opened the door and was off to light the first fuse of Civil War II.

Joe watched her black-clad figure stroll toward the pickup truck. A lamp further down the street silhouetted the subtle curve of her hip. He wondered—for the two-hundredth time—about the nature of her relationship with Beach. They seemed very friendly with one another, but then there was their age difference and the fact that Beach was Clare's boss. She seemed unfettered, and Joe—disconnected from his own wife by half the earth's circumference—was attracted to her like a tentative, lovesick puppy.

When she got close to the truck, he pushed the button on the radio and said: "All's clear."

She pulled the cylinder from her bag and stooped to set it below the truck—directly beneath the gas tank, as he had told her to do. He could see the tiny flicker of flame from her lighter: once, twice, a third time. Then another shadow, accompanied by a smaller, four legged shadow, appeared farther down the street.

Joe pushed the button on the radio. "Hold and stay down. We got a dog walker."

Clare's ninja-esque form disappeared under the truck. The person—man or woman, it was unclear—strolled toward them, leisurely, puffing on a cigarette and leading a fluffy, brown dog on a leash. The dog crapped in a yard. Its owner looked around and kept walking. Soon, owner and dog were directly beside the pickup truck. The dog growled. Its owner tugged the leash and kept walking. They soon rounded a corner and were out of sight.

Joe pushed the button again. "Stay put for a few more minutes in case they come back your way. I'll let you know when it's clear."

The radio crackled and Clare whispered, "I almost shit my pants."

They waited in silence, until the red glow of the cigarette reappeared. Dog and owner walked directly past the truck again and then back up the street from where they had come.

"Okay, light it up."

Another flicker of the lighter: this time the fuse caught. Clare's shadow emerged from beneath the truck. She walked briskly back to the van. Joe started the motor before she got there. As soon as she was inside he turned the wheel, leading them out of the neighborhood.

Just before they rounded the corner, an orange fireball exploded from beneath the truck. It rocked their van even though they were a thousand feet away. Joe stepped on the gas, careful not to skid the tires.

Clare pressed her face against the glass. "Holy shit, that was awesome!"

They all agreed it was awesome. They had left the "infidel's" truck a flaming wreck. They escaped Lynchburg without ever seeing an emergency vehicle or hearing a siren.

Joe set the cruise control directly on the posted speed limit. "Do you think we're ready to do a monument before we drive to West Virginia and find a place to spend the night?"

Fueled by adrenaline and a thermos of strong coffee, Joe drove them along the dark, lonely, back-roads to Charlottesville, the site of the Robert E. Lee statue where, during a protest, neo-Nazis had infamously killed a counter-protestor.

In Charlottesville they did a few circles around Emancipation Park, then backtracked until they found a wooded spot where they could hide the supplies that they didn't need for this operation. The spot would also serve as a place to rendezvous if something went wrong or if anyone was separated. When they returned to Emancipation Park, Joe pulled the van into a funeral parlor's parking lot and they studied the scene.

The park and its surrounding streets were deserted, but also well lit, meaning that anyone who happened to drive by would see them.

Joe pulled a silenced .22 pistol from one of his bags. The silencer was made with a perforated pipe within another, larger pipe, with holes drilled in each end. One side was threaded and screwed onto the gun's barrel. Between the pipes was steel wool to catch the escaping gasses when the gun fired to help muffle the noise.

Beach put a hand on Joe's shoulder. "I thought we all agreed there would be no guns."

Joe grinned. "We actually agreed there'd be *no hurting anyone*. We didn't say anything about guns, per se."

"He's got you there," Clare said.

"Trust me." Before Beach could stop him, Joe got out of the car, tucked the gun in his pants, and strolled across to the park. In the center, astride a metal horse, illuminated with spotlights, loomed Robert E. Lee, the revered General of the Confederacy. Joe pulled out his gun, aimed at the closest light, held his breath, and squeezed the trigger. The light went out. The statue got dimmer. The discharge sounded no louder than someone coughing. He picked up the spent shell casing and shot out eight more lights in the same manner, until the statue was shrouded in darkness. He then returned to the car, where the others were discussing the morality of destroying statues.

Beach was twisted around, addressing Clare in the backseat. "If you're concerned we're washing over history, these monuments were erected in an attempt to romanticize the South's legacy of state-sponsored human trafficking."

Joe climbed in and stashed the pistol under the seat. "If people want to jerk off to images of Robert E. Lee, they can still do it with a history book."

"That's not what I meant," Clare said. "I just meant that someone made this statue. Even though its message is ugly, isn't it still art?"

FD was fiddling with the settings on the plasma cutter. "Clare's right. It's definitely art." He looked up at her. "But think about the statues of Stalin and Saddam Hussein getting pulled down, or that portrait of Hitler with a bayonet slash across his face. By destroying all that shit, it takes on more meaning than when it's just bullshit fascist propaganda."

"I hadn't thought about it like that," Clare said. "By destroying art we're making *better* art."

Moral dilemma resolved, Clare remained in the van while Joe and Beach took up lookout positions at the northern and southern ends of the park. Joe turned a corner and walked casually down a side street. He then rounded a building, turned back via an alley, and hid behind a dumpster. From there he had a good view of the street and the park. A car passed, and then all was quiet. They each announced that the coast was clear, and it was ten minutes before Joe saw a white light and sparks appear near the statue.

FD had not been working more than five minutes when Beach announced, "Cop!"

The bright light went out, but Joe could still make out a dull orange glow, probably where the metal of the statue was still hot. The cop car stopped on the street about two hundred feet from Joe's position. Its mounted spotlight flicked on and cast a beam of light into the park.

The light swiped across the park, over hedges, past park benches, some trees. When it reached the statue's base, it stopped monetarily. Joe couldn't see what the cop could see, because they were looking into the park from different angles. He held his breath. Then the circle of light rose up as if it were a balloon and enveloped the entire statue. Robert E. Lee and his horse, framed by the spotlight, remained perfectly intact.

But within the light's frame was now plainly visible a black-clad man, straddling the horse behind General Lee. The man was masked and had the nozzle of a plasma cutter in one hand, the grounding cable clipped to the bill of the General's hat. With his dark safety glasses on, FD looked like a giant, black space alien.

The car's siren blipped and the lights flashed red and blue. The spotlight remained on FD, who casually unclipped the grounding cable from the hat and gave the head a good push.

The statue's head, mostly severed at the neck, folded forward. FD had already cut through it, except for a sliver of molten metal. With a determined shove, the head rolled off, struck the horse with a clang that echoed throughout the square, and tumbled into the darkness below the statue's base. The cop leapt from his car, drew his gun, and ran into the park.

FD dove off the horse and shot off like a bullet in the other direction. The cop ran after him. The area around the statue was now vacant.

Joe leapt from behind the dumpster and sprinted across the street to the park. Out of the corner of his eye he saw Beach hop into the cop car. When Joe got to the statue, the spotlight shot across the park. The cop car squealed down the street. Its siren wailed.

"Ayeeeeeee!" Beach screamed into the radio.

When Joe reached the statue, he picked up the severed head. It weighed about thirty pounds. FD had left the plasma cutter sitting on the base. Joe needed help if he was going to bring it, too, back to the van. He dropped the head on the pavement with a clank and pressed the radio's button. "Need help, quick!"

"On my way!" Clare said.

He looked again at the statue and had an idea. He pushed the button again. "Bring a bomb."

Sirens wailed far in the distance as he climbed atop the base. He attached the grounding cable to the hilt of the statue's sword and shot a beam of plasma straight into General Lee's ass. With no safety glasses, he kept his eyes screwed shut. His work was not pretty, but it didn't need to be.

But then he singed his thumb with the molten plasma. The pain almost knocked him off the statue. He looked at his glove, and he could see where his bare skin, melted and bubbling, was showing through the fabric. A drop of blood fell onto the base.

"Shit!"

He pulled his thumb out of the glove and held it against his palm to stem the bleeding.

"Joe!" Clare appeared below and handed up one of the bombs.

He took it with his good hand and wedged one end into the hole he had melted in the General's ass. He then bent the fuse gently toward the metal—careful not to put a kink in it—and blipped the torch into the grounded statue to light the fuse.

When the fuse began to sparkle, he leapt off the horse and snatched its severed head. Clare grabbed the plasma cutter. Together they ran back to the van. Police lights flashed on the other side of the square, and they reached the van just as the bomb exploded. The fireball lit up the park, but they didn't stick around to watch it.

Joe backed the van out of the funeral parlor's parking lot, rounded a corner, zigzagged away from the park, and pulled into an apartment complex. He killed the motor, pulled off his glove, and examined his thumb. It was not as bad as he thought, although he had burned a small patch of his skin off below his left knuckle. It felt like it was still on fire.

"Oh, my God!" Clare said. "Are you okay?"

"I'm fine. It's just a flesh wound."

She helped him wrap it in a t-shirt as they listened to the radio for signs of FD and Beach. All was eerily quiet.

When she finished tying off the bandage she leaned back in her seat and sighed loudly. "Do you think they're okay?"

"I think so… Listen, if anyone comes we should probably make out like we're lovers." She nodded. "I can't believe Beach stole the fucking cop car!"

She laughed uneasily. "Beach will be okay, one way or another. He's one of the cleverest men I've ever met. I'm more worried about Ef-dee. He… stands out more around here, and he's on foot."

"Yeah, but he had a big head start on that first cop, and they never saw his face." Joe reached over and squeezed one of her hands. "Are *you* okay?"

She nodded, wiped away a tear, and leaned her head onto his shoulder. He put an arm around her as she closed her eyes.

They stayed like that in silence for about twenty minutes, until their radios crackled. "I lost them." It was Beach's voice. "I wrapped the car around a tree, hurt my neck a bit—but I'm okay."

Clare snatched the radio from the console. "Thank God! Have you seen… the other person?"

"I guess we really need to come up with codenames," Joe muttered.

"Nada," Beach said.

They agreed to meet at the rendezvous point in the morning. Clare put her head back on Joe's shoulder. Soon he, too, closed his eyes and eventually fell asleep. Appropriately enough, he dreamed he was being chased, but it was not by cops: he was running from his father, who was racing after him with a belt around their old house.

He was startled awake by the radio. "Ace here. I was pinned down in a fucking dumpster all night, couldn't risk using the radio. That was some fancy driving—King. You sped right past me."

Clare shot up and broke into joyful tears. "Queen here. Get your asses to the rendezvous point. Let's get the hell out of this town. We've got more work to do."

"Copy that," Beach said. "Glad you're okay, Ace."

Joe sighed in relief and turned on the ignition. "I guess that makes me Jack… Jack the Fearless Vampire Killer. I sort of like the sound of that."

"Me too," she said.

8. White Shirts

So gifted at identifying other people's secret motivations, Clare Swan, notorious Queen of the Fearless Vampire Killers, was mystified by her own. When she graduated from law school, punching someone—even a Nazi—seemed like such a big deal. For someone who had lived a relatively sheltered life before college (she was a virgin until seventeen), lying to her parents, smoking ungodly amounts of weed, sleeping with her boss, fucking strangers at his request, retail sabotage, biological warfare: all of these transgressions had seemed like such a big deal at the time. But since she spent the better part of two weeks cutting the heads off Confederate statues across the South, her earlier misbehaviors seemed so innocent by comparison. On her first day back to Beach's office after a weekend with her parents in Vermont, her chest still reeled with the abandon of someone whose heart was disconnected completely from her head.

Her parents, such intellectuals, had always encouraged her to question the American metanarrative, that prism through which we view all things. She was aware that others, upon meeting the Fearless Vampire Killers, would place its members in categories. Beach was a middle-aged, divorcee alcoholic going through a mid-life crisis. Joe was a southern ex-pat estranged from his family who loathed his roots. FD was an underprivileged African American fed up with racism—immensely gifted, complex. Of course, with her eye for the unseen, she saw more than these superficialities. She felt their inner pain, and she wanted to help them. She felt responsible for Beach's vulnerability as if his heart lived between her teeth. She wanted to soothe Joe's self-loathing, whatever the cause. Her heart ached for FD's sadness, which she yearned to help him forget. But although Clare could feel all these things—and she knew how other people would likely describe her—she lacked awareness of her own inner pain.

She took another hit on her vape pen, closed the brief she was working on, and pulled up the news on her phone.

The public's reaction to their attacks was about what she had expected. Just like the 2016 election, the American population was divided into three, roughly equal groups: those who applauded them, those who condemned them, and those who were either too lazy or ill informed to voice an opinion. For two weeks, the news had covered virtually nothing else. Last weekend, even her parents guardedly admired the attackers, unaware that one of them was sitting right there. But if the public's reaction to the attacks was to be expected, the government's response was downright shocking for its swiftness and punitive nature.

Within seventy-two hours of their first attacks in Lynchburg and Charlottesville, President Mike Pence announced the creation of a new agency under the Department of Homeland Security called the "Alt-Left Terrorism Task Force." A former-colonel-turned-pastor who had been kicked out of the Army for sexual harassment, Stanley Congdon, was appointed czar, pending approval from the Senate. Cops from across the country were being detailed to fill the new agency. There were reports that these recruits were drawn heavily from members of "Cops for Comeup-Pence," the fascist police club. Meanwhile, the Task Force solicited public volunteers for a militia that would be used to flush out "leftwing extremists" from their havens in the major cities of the West and Northeast. Of course, skinheads and other rightwing lunatics immediately lined up at recruitment stations throughout the South. These volunteers, known informally as the "white shirts," were now being bused all over the country for impromptu "parades" in various progressive cities.

An article caught her eye: D.C.'s parade was today. It was 12:20 p.m. The white shirts were downtown at that moment, just a few blocks from Beach's office.

"They're throwing us a parade today!" she called to Beach in the other room. "Do you wanna go check it out?"

Since they returned to D.C., he had been obsessed with elevating Civil War II to the next level: a grand attack in the North. She had been sleeping at his house less frequently because he was too busy researching plans for some medieval siege engine he wanted to build. She would be worried about his sanity if that were not so hypocritical, given her own enthusiasm for the anti-fascist cause.

He appeared in his doorway with his cloak draped over his shoulders. "Nobody—literally *nobody*—likes parades except Nazis."

"What about Mardi Gras? I've always wanted to go to New Orleans."

"You think Mardi Gras is about parades? Kids like beads. Grownups like booze and tits." He smiled broadly. "You look beautiful, but I don't want to watch the occupation."

"Okay, but if I get arrested I expect you to come bail me out."

He kneeled in front of the couch and put his hand on her thighs. "Do you love me?"

"Maybe." She pressed her knees together.

He raised his eyebrows and slid his hands up her yoga pants until they reached her hipbones. "Do you love Ef-dee?"

She laughed. "No."

"Joe? He definitely has a hard-on for you."

"He's already married, and he's demented."

"We're all demented." He rested his head on her lap. "You know I don't care who you fuck, but I hope you'll always come back to me."

She ran her fingers through his hair. "I know."

"And don't punch anyone today." He kissed both her knees, stood, and marched back to his office. "We're going to hit them again soon enough!"

She was melancholy as she walked the few blocks to Constitution Avenue. She wished Beach had come with her, and she worried that their relationship had shifted in some imperceptible way. She suspected he felt threatened by Joe or FD. Besides mild flirting, nothing had happened between her and either of them, even though they had spent two weeks living together in the wilderness. Did Beach have any reason to be concerned?

She heard shouting ahead as she crossed Pennsylvania Avenue, and when she rounded the corner of the National Archives building there was a spattering of protesters around Constitution Avenue. When she reached the line of protestors, standing between the Archives—home of the U.S. Constitution—and the Department of Justice building, she caught her first glimpse of the white shirts. They were all white men wearing red hats, which were emblazed with "Make America Great Again!" They carried clubs and wore identical khaki pants and white golf shirts, on which were pinned tin badges identifying them as deputized militiamen of the Alt-Left Terrorism Task Force.

Just above, the blue flag of Justice waved mockingly: "Qui Pro Domina Justitia Sequitur."

Clare saw a few police officers sprinkled in with the white shirts. When she recognized Officer Meyer among them, she ducked behind another protestor until he passed.

The parade exuded no joy. The white shirts, sneering, angry men, marched not in lockstep, but along the periphery of the protestors, daring them to step out of line. A white shirt whose obese gut strained the fabric of his golf shirt raised his club menacingly in Clare's direction.

"Behold, the master race!" chided a protestor nearby.

The white shirt leapt into the crowd, swung his club at the taunting protestor, missed, and fell flat on his face. Other white shirts, clubs flailing, charged the protestors, who scattered. Clare jumped backwards. Beside her another protestor fell and was swarmed by the white shirts, who beat him with their clubs. There were no police to stop them.

Rather, these thugs *were* the police.

She turned to run away but one of the white shirts grabbed her arm, spun her around, and punched her right in the mouth. She fell to the ground. A steel-toed boot struck her ribs, knocking the wind out of her. She curled into a ball, prepared to have her brains beat onto the sidewalk.

"Not her!" said a commanding voice. "She's one of us!"

Still gasping for air, she opened an eye and peered beneath her folded arms. She realized one of her teeth had come loose. A man stood above her, grinning, muscular arms at his sides. She didn't recognize him at first, but gradually it dawned on her who it was; he was one of the men she met on Craigslist, the guy she fucked at the Trump International Hotel: Garth Simonson, the project manager who worked for Backwater Mercenaries. Garth offered his hand and lifted her off the ground. He wore the same getup as the white shirts, except he had a whistle around his neck. He was a former Marine, square-jawed, powerfully built, but as she recalled, he had the smallest dick she had ever seen.

"Holy shit!" Clare said when she finally caught her breath. Her lip stung. She touched her loose tooth—a lateral incisor. It wiggled like a light switch. Her fingers drew back blood. "What the fuck?"

"My company got the contract to organize these hooligans." He chuckled and familiarly brushed away some dirt on her yoga pants. "Sorry they roughed you up a bit. They're still a little undisciplined, but we're working on that. Believe me, it was no easy task to organize a parade like this in just a few days..."

The protestors had all been chased away, and now Clare and Garth were just two acquaintances chatting on the street. Her side ached and she felt nauseous. She clenched her fist, about to punch her second Nazi, when she remembered Beach's words: "We're going to hit them again soon enough." Garth might come in handy. She loosened her fist, swallowed the blood, and listened to him prattle on.

"Hey," he said at last. "I've got a room at the Hay-Adams tonight, if you want to get together later."

She forced a closed-lipped smile. "The Hay-Adams?"

"Yeah, the Trump Hotel doesn't have any rooms at the moment." He leaned forward and lowered his voice to a whisper. "I heard they gotta bedbug problem."

"I can't tonight, Garth, but let's do it again soon."

"Awesome. The only catch is that I just accepted a gig at the White House, so I don't know if I'll be staying in many hotels after I start my new job."

"The White House?"

"Yeah, working under the Task Force's czar. The President knows the only way to fight an insurgency is if the Task Force stays with the locals, so I'll be overseeing the Washington Region." He held the whistle up to his lips. "I'm glad we bumped into each other. Sorry again about my volunteers."

"I'll live." Clare choked back her vomit. "Message me."

He blew the whistle, and the white shirts returned to Constitution Avenue to resume their march. Garth barked orders, winked at Clare, and the parade moved off down the street toward the U.S. Capitol. She had been only twelve the last time she looked into eyes so devoid of empathy, when her cousin molested her on his living room couch. She watched the fascists' triumphant departure, then threw up on the sidewalk.

9. Valuable Property

Like all lifelong Washingtonians, Beach had grown accustomed to his city's perpetual occupation. D.C. residents were gerrymandered into a legislative black hole during its creation, circa 1790: no congressional representation, citizens subject to the whims—however insane—of the various states' residents. But despite having lived here for forty-eight years, he never witnessed an occupation so overt as an army of federally deputized neo-Nazis with clubs marching down Constitution Avenue. When Clare returned to his office with beautiful lips swollen, missing her front tooth, rib bruised, Beach set fire to his law books in the center of his office, drank three martinis, pissed out the fire, and called for an emergency meeting of the Fearless Vampire Killers. A mad plan had been percolating in his head since they returned to D.C., and now was the time for action.

The next day—large messenger bag pregnant with hammer, crowbar, flashlight, construction helmets—he struggled to keep up with Clare as they rode their bikes from Super Court, where he had had a mid-morning status hearing, to Union Station. Even though she was injured and carrying half of their equipment, he could still hardly keep up with her. In a strange way, her missing incisor made her even more alluring to him. So far she had resigned not to replace the tooth, but to wear the gap like a badge of honor.

They locked their bikes outside and waited for FD and Joe, who arrived at precisely the same time: 11:15 a.m. Whatever their idiosyncrasies, they were punctual. There were greetings, hugs, and talk of the white shirts and Clare's swollen lip. Beach handed out blue helmets and orange vests, and they meandered by foot down to Capitol Hill via Massachusetts Avenue. They carried their helmets. It was a lovely day for a walk.

"So King," Joe said, when they had covered a couple blocks, "when are you going to tell us about your grand plan?"

Beach grinned. "There's some real estate I want to show you."

Clare laughed. Joe scratched his head. FD looked skeptical.

Once they reached Stanton Park, Beach led them right, south, zigzagging through a quiet neighborhood of extremely rich residences and the businesses that catered to them. He pointed out a house, now a museum, where Frederick Douglass once lived. They turned left, then right, then right again.

When he found what he was looking for, Beach stopped and gestured to an abandoned home surrounded by a construction fence. "Prepare yourselves for perhaps the most harebrained scheme ever concocted by someone with revolutionary inclinations."

The others donned their helmets and gawked at Beach's "real estate" interest.

It was of the ubiquitous, brownstone variety, the style built primarily in the 1920's and found all over D.C., lined up like books on a shelf. This particular brownstone, nothing but a dilapidated shell, stood entirely on its own: a hollow, upright book with no pages and no neighbors, alone in the middle of a large, vacant lot. The windows and doors were boarded up. The roof had apparently caved in a long time ago, leaving the inside open to the elements. Clearly it was either slated for demolition, or someone was planning on keeping the brick shell and redoing the interior. The land itself, given its proximity to the U.S. Capitol, was highly valuable.

Helmeted, vested, gloved, doing their best to look like innocuous construction-types, they scooted through a hole in the fence and used a crowbar to pry open the plywood that served as the backdoor. The wood came apart easily, as Beach had been inside before, while Clare was in Vermont. He scurried in first, climbing on hands and knees atop a mountain of debris until he found a spot stable enough to stand upright. Except for a thick beam running the length of the house, the second level—including the joists, the staircase, and the floor itself—had long ago fallen down. He brushed off the suit he still wore from court and looked up at the sky as the others, one by one, joined him.

"So, what's the plan?" FD said once they were all inside.

Beach reached into his bag and pulled out the pages of designs he had printed from the internet. He handed FD a flashlight. "You're the artist and the engineer among us. I want you to build us a giant trebuchet, right here."

"A tray-boo what?"

"A trebuchet. It's a type of siege engine—sort of like a catapult—that was used in the Middle Ages to knock down castle walls. It uses a counterweight to hurl stones a long distance." Beach passed around a printed out street-view of where they were. "See, East Capitol Street points directly at the Capitol. This house is built on this side street, just off East Capitol, meaning that the Capitol dome is just a few blocks directly that way"—he pointed toward the backdoor—"just beyond the U.S. Supreme Court."

"You know, I dropped outta engineering school…"

Clare smiled at FD. "I know you can do it."

FD studied the designs in silence for several minutes. "Maybe this could be done, but the math would have to be *extremely* precise."

"It's simple." Beach held up one of the diagrams. "Well, most of it is. We use the house as our frame. We just need another payload beam that pivots on an axle, a sling to carry the payload—and the counterweight, of course."

FD studied the structure. "Have you figured out how heavy the counterweight would have to be?"

"Three thousand pounds max."

Joe laughed. "That's almost as much as a car!"

Beach pulled out another page and handed it to Joe. "But that's throwing payload that weighs twenty-five pounds the length of *three* football fields. If we can lighten the payload or if the distance is less—which I think it is—we don't need as much weight."

FD studied the diagrams some more, passing each one to Joe when he was done. Joe studied them too and scratched his head. They walked around the house, plodding over piles of plaster and trash, being careful not to fall through the weatherworn floor into the basement. Clare entered what appeared to be the former kitchen and took pictures with an old-school digital camera. Beach watched them all, seeped in agitated contemplation. Why had it taken him nearly a half-century to find these brilliantly deranged people?

"Alright," FD said at last. "I think I can do it. We'd need some surveying equipment to get the distance and the trajectory right…"

"Can we build it by next Tuesday?" Beach asked.

Joe looked up from the diagrams. "What happens then?"

Clare stowed her camera and rejoined them. "That's when the Senate is having Stanley Congdon's confirmation hearing."

FD nodded. "Maybe."

Beach loosened his tie, removed a flask of gin from his jacket, and raised it to the sky. The passing clouds made him dizzy—or perhaps it was just his revolutionary fervor. "To retaking D.C." He took a swig and passed it around.

"*Our* city."

10. Capitol Siege

On the day his father's eyes closed for the last time, FD spent the night clandestinely painting a mural beneath the John Philip Sousa Bridge. It was a portrait of his father as FD remembered him in the days before his death, before his raspy breathing stopped and the machine keeping him alive began its wailing, futile alarm.

When a cop on the bridge yelled and shone a light down on him, he dove into the Anacostia River. Submerged in the currents that whisked him away, he screamed beneath the water in the agony of sorrow—and continued screaming, barely attempting to swim, until the river dumped him, like a corpse, at Anacostia Park. There, he pulled himself onto the grass, stared up at the sky, and tried to imagine what life would be like without his father. It was unfathomable.

Two years later, it was still unfathomable.

The following day, FD skipped school. He continued skipping for two weeks. His professors called him. He had been on the dean's list, on his way to becoming a brilliant engineer. Encouraged by his father, FD had once yearned to build something important and beautiful. He ignored his professors' calls. With his father gone he couldn't imagine anything more important and beautiful than a simple mural honoring his memory. And he didn't need to go to school for that.

Now, clad in a white Tyvek suit that covered him from head to toe, he admired his first engineering marvel. Was it beautiful? It was certainly *not* art, even in a loose sense, but there was beauty in its purpose. Was it important? Well, that depended on whether it worked or not. He was about to find out, for Stanley Congdon's confirmation hearing was scheduled to start in ten minutes.

Also in a Tyvek suit, mopping perspiration from his forehead with a rag, Beach read off an inventory of their captured Confederate heads. "Four Robert E. Lees, a Jefferson Davis, a John S. Mosby, two Stonewall Jacksons, a JEB Stuart, and a Nathan Bedford Forrest—"

"The Klan's first goddamned Grand Wizard," Clare said from atop the wooden ladder, which reached all the way to what had once been the attic.

"Right." Beach rolled over one of the Robert E. Lees with his Tyvek-shod toe.

"Don't forget the six anonymous soldiers' heads," FD said.

For the past week, Joe had meticulously hollowed out the inside of the heads with a Dremel tool, so each would weigh exactly twenty pounds. This decreased the counterweight they needed. It was Clare who realized, once she climbed the ladder, that from the roof they could see the tip of the slave-built "Statue of Freedom" standing atop the Capitol dome. Using a laser distance finder and a surveyor's theodolite, they aligned their trebuchet perfectly with the crest of feathers on the statue's helmet and knew the distance down to a few feet.

"Jack, you copy?" Clare said into the radio.

"Copy," Joe's voice replied into their earpieces. "I'm in position. Just give me a heads up—harhar—and fire away."

FD took another moment to admire his masterpiece. As a counterweight they had used nearly fifty flat, iron plates strapped into a metal harness he had welded together himself. The plates were the kind commonly found in gyms, each weighing forty-five pounds. Altogether their counterweight was over two thousand pounds, which (he thought) was heavy enough to propel the bronze heads into the Capitol dome. The harness was designed so they could take out or add weight, as necessary, to make their missiles fall farther or shorter.

They couldn't, however, change the trajectory, since the trebuchet was built into the shell of the house. In order to align their payload beam—a repurposed, thirty-foot light pole—with the dome, they had had to build it slightly off kilter from the frame of the house. If any part of his calculations were wrong, they would miss the dome every time, and there was nothing they could do about it.

Clare came down the ladder. "Are you guys sure these things aren't going to hit someone?"

FD loaded one of Robert E. Lee heads into the trebuchet's sling. "I'm not sure of nothing, but the dome's made of cast iron and we're a long way away."

"If we kill anyone it will be God's fault," Beach said.

"You don't believe in God."

"All the same."

Clare shrugged and walked to the backdoor. Unlike FD and Beach, she was wearing workout clothes. "I'll take my place now." She disappeared behind the plywood.

As Clare got settled into her lookout spot down the block, FD and Beach turned the trebuchet's wench. The arms of the wench were six-feet, steel stop-sign tubes, providing the leverage to lift the great weight. With one person using his bodyweight to pull downward, and the other pushing upward on the other side with all his strength, they painstakingly lifted the counterweight until it was at a forty-five-degree angle from the payload beam. Once there, FD placed a hook onto the end of the beam, which spanned the length of the house.

"Queen in position," came Clare over the radio. "All clear."

"Copy that," Joe said.

FD held the sledgehammer out to Beach. "This was your idea, so you should take the first swing."

Beach waved his hand. "Please, this is your creation. You go first."

FD hefted the hammer over his shoulder, preparing to swing and knock the hook loose from the beam. At that, the counterweight would drop, the payload beam would shoot through the roof, and the sling would release the head, which would then soar nearly eight hundred feet—hopefully straight through the Capitol dome.

Beach stood clear and held the radio's button down: "One head of Robert E. Lee, traitor, notorious human trafficker, failed general— we reject thee, fake history. Return to sender."

FD swung the hammer. The weight dropped with a whoosh. General Lee's head was pitched through the ceiling. Despite the awesome force, it was surprisingly quiet because the payload beam pivoted on an axel with well-oiled bearings. The sling, now empty, dangled from the side of the house where the kitchen had once been. Besides some dust kicked up by the movement, it was dead still.

They looked at each other wide-eyed and smiled, waiting to hear if their attack was a success. It took about thirty seconds.

"Holy shit," Joe said. "You overshot the Dome by about two hundred feet. The head landed in a fountain. It made a helluva splash—but I don't think anyone saw it."

FD climbed the ladder, unthreaded an arm on the harness, and wiggled one of the weights free. He passed it down to Beach, who set it against the wall. FD then refastened the harness and came down the ladder. They again cranked up the counterweight, and FD set the hook. Then they loaded Jefferson Davis' head into the sling.

Beach lifted the sledgehammer as FD announced into the radio that another shot was coming. Beach swung. The engine sprung a second time. They waited.

"It landed on the pavement," Joe said.

FD pushed the button. "Distance?"

"Hundred feet, maybe. The thing is lodged in the cement. I can't quite see it from here, but I think it got someone's attention... There's a Capitol Police officer walking over that way now..."

FD was already handing another weight down to Beach. "This should do it." He refastened the harness and leapt down from the ladder.

"He's staring at the ground," Joe continued. "Now he's looking around and calling someone on his radio. He doesn't seem to have any idea what it is or where it came from."

They furiously turned the crank until the counterweight was back in position. Beach loaded one of the Stonewall Jacksons into the sling.

FD snatched the sledgehammer and turned to Beach. "We don't have too many more tries before they figure out they're under attack—and then they're going to start trying to figure out where we are."

"Fuck the world."

FD swung. The engine lunged. They waited.

"Direct hit!" Joe said. "It bounced right off the dome. There's no way they didn't hear that inside."

FD and Beach screamed victory, but as they had many more heads to shoot and not a lot of time, they jumped back to work immediately. They worked the wench and loaded the heads as fast as they could. But because they no longer needed to adjust the weights, it was only seventeen minutes before they shot all their anonymous soldiers, the other three Robert E. Lees, the John S. Mosby, the other Stonewall Jackson, and the JEB Stuart. Joe reported that some of the heads broke through the dome. Others ricocheted off. It didn't matter. Police ran about everywhere, like ants whose mound had been disturbed. Soon lawmakers and their aides sprinted from every door as the Capitol was evacuated. The czar's hearing would have to be postponed: such a shame.

FD was about to load their last head, the Nathan Bedford Forrest, when Clare's voice came on the radio: "Hold on. You've got a cop driving by out front."

Once they stopped working, they could hear sirens outside, lots of them. Beach was panting, out of breath, but he was smiling like a little boy on his birthday. FD smiled back, but they remained perfectly still.

It was three minutes before Clare said, "He's gone. He asked me if I saw anything unusual. They're looking for a plane or a drone."

They cranked the counterweight for the last shot. Beach latched the hook and handed the hammer to FD. "The final head's yours, Ace."

Beach held the radio button down: "Last up, Nathan Bedford Forrest: terrorist, traitor, war criminal. May ye rot in hell—*forever*."

FD grinned, swung the hammer, and the Grand Wizard's head flew through the air. Before Joe informed them that it smashed straight through the dome, FD and Beach were pouring gasoline on the debris around the trebuchet and the walls. They pulled off their Tyvek suits, stuffed them in a plastic bag, and scooted out the plywood backdoor. FD took one last look at his accomplishment. Perhaps it *was* art. He was sad to watch it burn. Beach lit the gasoline by the door when they were clear, and they walked to meet Clare at the rendezvous spot.

As the shrill scream of sirens filled the city, FD recalled the sound of the alarm that had signaled his father's death. He thought he would die that day too, but he had kept on living. As Clare greeted him with a warm embrace and he felt her lithe body pressed against his, he couldn't recall a time when he had been happier. Like a phoenix, he had risen from the ashes of despair and was now an integral part of something that would be remembered forever.

But what did the sirens now herald for the ALT Task Force? It was certainly not the death knell for American fascism, which had weathered so many defeats and scandals it now seemed like a forgone conclusion. More likely, President Pence would use their attack as an excuse to clamp down harder. The thought made FD's blood run cold.

11. Hornet's Nest

A plume of smoke wafted into the sky beyond the U.S. Capitol dome, which had cracked like an eggshell under the sustained barrage of Confederate heads. Joe, whose own head was so full of things he longed to forget, wished for once that he could snap a picture to remember the scene forever. Redemption never looked so glorious. But switching on his phone was out of the question. When a couple white shirts began to walk his way, he got on his bike and casually zoomed off across the National Mall.

Police vehicles from every agency imaginable choked Constitution Avenue: MPD, FBI, Capitol Police, Park Police, Secret Service, Federal Protective Services, Metro Transit Police, Postal Police, Department of Homeland Security, and of course a few shiny new vans of the Alt-Left Terrorism Task Force. Civilian traffic was halted, vehicles searched, but Joe passed on his bicycle with no problem. Fifty soldiers, machine guns in the low ready, stood on the White House lawn. Behind them loomed a tank—a fucking tank! Its main gun was pointed at eye level. Joe held his breath as he passed.

"Shit, we really kicked a hornet's nest," he said under his breath.

Tourists were being ordered off the Lincoln Memorial, which was cordoned off with crime scene tape. Joe rounded the Memorial onto Arlington Memorial Bridge. A gaggle of police cars blocked the lanes, but in the confusion he was able to slip by using the sidewalk. He had planned on dropping his radio off this bridge into the Potomac, but there was no way he could do that now. He coasted down the bike path on Washington Boulevard—traffic at a dead stop due to the roadblocks—past the Pentagon Memorial, and onto Columbia Pike. Another two miles and he turned onto his street. He sighed in relief when he saw his blue Corolla parked in front of the garage.

But there were two black shoes sticking out from beneath the car.

Joe wheeled his bike into a neighbor's driveway—trying to seem casual—and rang the bell. He kept one eye on his car. Soon a buzz-cut cop-type emerged from beneath it, looked around conspiratorially, brushed his hands on his jeans, and walked to an awaiting car: a gray sedan, American, otherwise nondescript. Although the man was not in uniform, Joe recognized the blond hair and pugnacious profile of Officer Meyer. Joe's skin boiled where his tattoos had once been.

"Joe!" The beaming, crinkled face of Ms. Rosa, last name unknown, opened the door and shooed him inside. "How is Naagesh? He must be so big now! And Geeta? Did you hear what happened today?"

Joe stooped to pet her dog, named Harry Belafonte (or just "Harry" for short), a black Havanese. He glanced once more to see the gray sedan creep down the block and around the corner. Ms. Rosa shut the door, and they sat on the couch together for an hour, sipping hibiscus tea and chitchatting about topics as far ranging as Rosa's late husband and 9-11. When he felt it was safe again to go out, Joe thanked her for the tea, pledged to drop by again soon, and pushed his bike across the street to his house.

Although he knew there was now a GPS tracker attached to his car, there were no obvious signs of surveillance on the street. The gray sedan was gone. Had they entered his house too with a no-knock warrant? He didn't think so. Even if they did, there was nothing incriminating there, except for his tools, but there was nothing illegal about owning tools. He had meticulously scrubbed away any trace of evidence. They had all been so careful. So, why was he under surveillance?

He took a shower and then called FD from his burner phone while the water was still running. He told FD what happened, and they agreed on a place where they could meet and discuss what to do next.

Joe then donned two layers of clothes, switched on his iPhone, got in his Corolla, and drove a meandering route through Fairfax County toward Dulles Airport. He periodically made erratic lane changes and U-turns. He looked continually in his mirror, but he saw no signs of the surveillance he knew must be there. Either the ALT Task Force guys were very good, or they were hanging back and just tracking him with the GPS tracker. Just to be certain, he pulled over on the side of the Dulles Toll Road for a full two minutes, letting everyone speed past him.

When he got to the airport he jerked his car into the short-term parking lot and ran into the airport. There he entered a bathroom and inconspicuously dropped his iPhone—silenced, but power on—into the bag of someone at a urinal. Then he bought a ticket, using his real name and credit card, for a Tampa flight leaving in an hour. He went through security and spent ten minutes perusing books in the bookstore. Pretending to be interested in something on a bottom shelf, he took off his outer layer of clothing and crawled out another entrance—then darted out of the secure area, out of the airport, and jumped into a hotel shuttle.

With his fake ID and a wad of cash, he checked into a hotel. He was soon sprawled on one of two queen-size beds watching CNN, certain there was no way they could have followed him there. By now they likely figured out he never got on the plane to Tampa, and they would chase his iPhone signal across the country.

He absorbed the news. Stanley Congdon was confirmed anyway as the czar of the ALT Task Force. They had had to violate the Senate rules, but it was unlikely the Supreme Court, in the President's pocket, would object. Damage to the Capitol was estimated to be in the millions. One side was dented in like a ping-pong ball. Various legislative spokespersons gnashed their teeth. Pundits pontificated.

"Fuck them all," Joe said to himself, just as there was a knock on the door.

It was the rest of the Fearless Vampire Killers. He let them in. There were weary congratulations. FD sat on the still-made bed. Joe returned to his spot on the other bed. Clare tossed her vape pen to Joe and disappeared into the bathroom. Beach remained standing by the door.

"Don't worry, man." FD had brought a sketchpad and was drawing a picture of Clare with her missing tooth. "I'm sure it's just Meyer has it out for you about the break-in."

"Ef-dee's right." Beach kept his hand on the door's lever. "If they really had anything on you they'd have arrested you already. The fact that he put a tracker on your car—probably without a warrant—means he's got *nothing*."

"I hope you're both right." Joe took a hit of Clare's weed. On the TV, Mr. Congdon was waxing about "how to eat soup with a knife." Joe changed the channel.

"Even so," Beach said. "I think we should all lay low for a while."

Joe acknowledged that that was probably a good idea. The others had already discussed it on their way out to Dulles. They would split up for six weeks and then get together again to plan another attack once things cooled off.

Beach opened the door. "I'm going to find us some liquor."

"We're in Virginia," Joe said. "They only sell hard liquor at government-owned ABC stores."

"Fucking puritans. The only thing worse than a bedbug is a fucking puritan."

When Beach was gone, Joe looked at the closed bathroom door, turned up the TV volume slightly, stood, and sat beside FD. His picture of Clare was beautiful. "Can I ask you a question, confidentially?"

"Confidentially?"

"Yeah." Joe handed the vape pen to FD, who took a long drag and set his drawing on the nightstand. "Do you trust these two?" Joe asked. "You remember how friendly that prosecutor was with Clare in the courtroom after the hearing?"

FD exhaled and handed him back the vape pen. "Beach and Clare have been with us every step o' the way. They're just as culpable as we are." He glanced at the bathroom door. "If there's anything that worries me a bit it's Beach's drinking."

His lungs full of weed, Joe exhaled to respond when the bathroom door swung open and Clare appeared. She was wearing ripped jeans and a black tank top. "What are you guys talking about?" She passed by the empty bed and climbed between them.

Joe made room and handed her the vape pen. "If I ask you something, do you promise not to take it the wrong way?" he asked.

"Promise." She pulled a vial from her jeans and reloaded the pen.

"What's up with you and Beach?"

"Our relationship is... open." She took a long hit and passed the pen to FD.

"But there is a relationship?" Joe asked.

"More or less."

She then laughed, crossed her arms, and lifted the tank top over her head in one motion, tossing it on the floor beside the bed. She wore no bra. She was all ribs and shoulders. He and FD could have played catch with her like a paper airplane. Joe nearly fell off the bed.

In his mind, already impinged with the consciousness-enhancing effects of weed, what happened next was a series of vivid snapshots. He and FD collided against Clare. More clothes were discarded. She bit FD's lip. Joe yanked off her jeans like they were on fire. He pulled her onto her hands and knees. He grabbed her hips. He pulled her hair. He fucked her like it was his last fuck before a lifetime of prison. She moaned with her lips around FD's cock.

He had just come and was wiping his dick off on the sheet, when Beach walked in with a grocery bag. Beach set the bag beside the sink, pulled out two bottles, and began to fix drinks as if there was nothing unusual going on.

"Want a martini, Joe? I bought some vermouth."

"Sure?" Joe searched for his underwear and pants on the floor.

Meanwhile, Clare had climbed atop FD and began riding him, moaning loudly, arms and torso flailing like an air dancer outside a carpet store. Joe pulled on his pants and sat on the other bed. Beach mixed their drinks and sat beside him. When Joe saw Beach's eyes glance at his scars, he put his shirt back on. FD tossed Clare, laughing, onto her back.

"You're really okay with this?" Joe said.

"Monogamy is a social construct."

Joe tried to imagine what he would feel like if it were Geeta on the other bed, her legs wrapped around another man. There was something profoundly unsettling about it, deep down in his male DNA. Even though he knew it made him a hypocrite—as he had just cheated on Geeta with Clare—the thought of his wife with someone else made his blood boil with jealousy. He suddenly wanted to be anywhere else but in that room, to be back in the wilderness, on the Appalachian Trail.

He stood and walked to the door, past the bed. "I'm going to get some ice."

"A southern gentleman." Beach's eyes, glassy, watched Clare and FD obliterate one another.

Joe nodded and left. Behind the door he could still hear Clare's rhythmic screams, as if she was being murdered inside. He kept walking down the hall, past the ice machine, until all was quiet, just him and his ghosts.

12. Shuffling the Deck

Clare woke the next morning, head throbbing, lip stuck to the pillow, Beach's arms draped around her shoulders, his body pressed against hers like a voluptuous, hairy spoon. Her pussy felt like it had been punched. Sunlight poured between a crack in the curtains, glimmering off dirty glasses, empty bottles, white sheets. They were alone. She vaguely recalled Joe leaving to get some ice; he never returned. When had FD left?

She had woken up like this on other occasions with Beach—post-debaucherous quietude—but on this morning she felt unsettled. Their previous Craigslist trysts were with enemies and strangers, men she would never see again, men she never desired to see again. But last night had been different. She was now certain—as she had not been before having sex with them—that she felt a special connection with FD and Joe, not merely as fellow revolutionaries, but as kindred, tortured souls. Now that they were gone, she worried her and Beach's proclivities had driven them away forever.

She nudged Beach. "Will you get me some ice?"

He squeezed her tighter and mumbled something incoherent, then begrudgingly stood, pulled on his boxers, shuffled out the door, and returned a few minutes later with a cup of ice. He set it on the nightstand and fell back onto the bed, eyes shut, his hand on her stomach, his beard nestled against her shoulder. Trying her best to let him sleep, she slowly removed one of the pillowcases, poured the ice inside to make a cold compress, and held it against her mons pubis. Nipples pointed at the ceiling, she turned on the news, volume off, closed captioning on.

On the screen, gums flapped silently, hands wrung impotently, and images of the damaged dome and the National Mall, now swarming with police and white shirts, flashed. The captions announced that a rightwing radio announcer, a well-known espouser of outlandish conspiracies, had been gunned down last night outside his studio. A pundit declared it was clearly the same group of "alt-left terrorists" responsible for the Capitol attack. Of course, this was impossible, as the soreness between Clare's legs attested. In any event, newly confirmed ALT Task Force czar Stanley Congdon, the former pastor, was going to address the nation in thirty minutes. His prayerful voice would reportedly heal the nation and make everything clear.

She pressed her tongue into her missing tooth's gap and recalled her chance meeting with Garth Simonson. He had obviously not known that her rib was cracked or that her tooth would fall out, but he had witnessed the assault. He had helped her off the ground. Her face had been smeared with blood. She knew he was a fascist before their first meeting at the Trump International Hotel, when she swiped his keycard to help infest the place with bedbugs. But his shocking lack of concern for her on Constitution Avenue had brought back memories that she had done her best to forget for the past fifteen years.

Her cousin Joshua had been eighteen, oily, a Young Republican about to head off to college. She was twelve, innocent, oblivious. She adored him and looked up to him. Even as he took off his pants and goaded her to touch him, he had made it seem like a game, which was why she played along. Before it progressed beyond touching, his mother—Clare's aunt on her mother's side—came home and caught them. Aunt Becky's reaction was to scream at Clare: "You get away from my son!"

A stern lecture followed: What Clare had done was not acceptable behavior for young ladies. It was the sort of thing a whore would do. Did she want to become a whore? Sobbing, Clare looked searchingly at Joshua's face, waiting for him to defend her. It had all been his idea; she had merely done what he asked her to do. She was not a whore! Before Joshua had initiated his "game" she had been playing with her English-style riding stable figures, minding her own business. The face that looked back at her was not the Joshua she knew: his jaw was set, his eyes cold. And then, behind Aunt Becky's back, he smiled.

It was not a friendly or supportive smile. It was a smile that Clare would recognize later in life as the mark of a sociopath. Bereft of compassion, consumed only with self-interest: he was smug because he had gotten away with something. Looking back, she had no doubt Joshua would have continued his "game" until he raped her, and for that reason alone she counted herself lucky. Her parents' reaction was to send her to therapy and not report Joshua to the police. He went to college and drowned the next year in a pool during a frat party. She gloated at his funeral. She made herself forget.

But she had not truly forgotten, and as she watched Mr. Congdon walking to a podium at the Rayburn House Office Building (the U.S. Capitol itself had not yet been deemed structurally sound) the cause of her inner pain, long buried within her hippocampus, glowed like a jellyfish, and she was able to trace its tendrils along the various choices of her adulthood—law school, protests, drugs, Beach, the Fearless Vampire Killers—into the hotel bed where she now lay holding a cold, soggy pillowcase between her legs.

Her parents, otherwise so supportive, had let her down. Her mother didn't want her nephew's life to be "ruined" for what must have been an "isolated impropriety." Clare's sociopathic cousin had used and humiliated her. But the worst part had been Aunt Becky's words. Years after the incident, Clare had questioned, perhaps subconsciously, whether she was, in fact, "a whore." Had she led Joshua on in some way? Had she "asked for it?" Later she recognized the absurdity of these questions; she had been twelve years old, for fuck's sake, and he was eighteen. Her aunt's "gut" (read, societally conditioned) reaction, the paternal hypocrisy, the slut shaming—it enraged Clare and caused her to rebel against the very notion of so-called "unacceptable behavior," for young ladies or anyone else. When she met Beach, resolutely perverted, she embraced his perversion because it seemed like a fitting "fuck you" to the metanarrative of American white male supremacy.

Yet, Beach was also a white male. He was also her boss.

She had assumed *she* was the dominant one in her and Beach's relationship—that it was her conscious choices that dictated their actions—but as she now followed the jellyfish's tendrils she wondered whether Beach, having sensed these strings that had theretofore remained hidden from her consciousness, was the one using her? He was highly intelligent and persuasive. Was she like a woman with "daddy issues" who had missed the underlying patterns and ended up marrying her daddy anyway?

He stirred and kissed her shoulder. "Last night was fun..."

"It was." She tossed the wet pillowcase on the floor and turned up the volume, hoping to force these troubling thoughts from her mind. "Congdon's about to give a speech about us."

Beach sat up and rubbed his eyes at the TV. "You know, my dear, I think maybe we shouldn't mix our pleasure with business anymore."

The czar, baldhead gleaming, waved to a few people off camera, his face set in a now-familiar, sociopathic grin, and then he cleared his throat into the microphones. "Mr. President, Mr. Speaker, Mr. President Pro Tempore, members of Congress, and fellow Americans. Last night we saw firsthand the work of Satan, right here in our nation's capital…"

"We don't really know Joe and Ef-dee well," Beach said. "Did you see Joe's scars?"

"Scars?"

"You were mostly turned the other way."

"They hate God," Mr. Congdon continued. "They hate freedom. This satanic scourge will stop at nothing until they have destroyed America and everything we stand for, until they have taken the last gun and until any girl can walk into a supermarket and get an abortion from a vending machine…"

Clare shut off the volume. "I can't listen to this shit."

"It's like being in church."

"More like hell."

"Same thing."

They followed along on the close captions, full of biblical references, jingoism, utter stupidity, dog whistles, war drums: Make America Great Again! The apogee, delivered in the same soulless smirk, was a declaration of martial law in Washington, D.C., as per the President's order. The white shirts would occupy an encampment on the National Mall to drive Satan from the city and "protect" the citizens from more attacks.

Beach shot from the bed, naked, flaccid penis bouncing. "A parade is one thing—but they can't *stay* in our city! I can't stand for it! I won't stand for it!"

As he ranted at the TV, Clare stood, found her clothes, got dressed, and sat back on the bed. When the czar's speech was over, President Mike Pence stood to reaffirm his declaration of martial law and to announce the appointment of a special counsel to reexamine the circumstances of Donald Trump's death. Beach sat heavily beside her, still gaping at the screen.

She studied his profile: martini gut, disheveled beard, and earnest gray eye, sclera slightly jaundiced. "We can't do anything, Beach. They may be onto Joe already, which means they could be watching us too. You said it yourself. We need to lay low for a while."

He waved a hand at the TV. "But the fucking Nazis are moving into Marseilles!"

"We're at the airport. We can buy tickets to somewhere and meet again in six weeks, like we all agreed." She put on her shoes.

"And abandon D.C.? Never!" His eyes never left the TV.

"You know, Beach, I'm going to take your advice about not mixing business and pleasure." She stood, kissed his forehead, and walked to the door, hand on the lever. "I think we should stop seeing each other."

He stood, still naked, singularly vulnerable, his hands extended in supplication. "Clare, don't go... I love you."

"I know."

She stepped out the door and cried all the way to the airport.

13. Beach Detoxes

With his heart ripped from his chest, Beach quit drinking cold turkey and returned to his regularly scheduled day job: defense attorney. He cleaned up the law-book bonfire he had made in his office, visited a few of his neglected clients at the D.C. jail, wrote motions, scheduled hearings, paid bills, and otherwise tried to forget about the fascist encampment on the National Mall just a few blocks away from his office. He also tried to take care of a few personal things he had neglected while he was off waging Civil War II. He washed the dishes piled in the sink and cleaned his bathroom (sans toilet). He scheduled an appointment with his doctor, a routine checkup, before his medical insurance was canceled, a casualty of malicious government intervention. He got a haircut. He visited his aging parents in Chevy Chase.

But at night, without Clare and without alcohol, he watched the news and simply stewed in his own misery. There were some more attacks on rightwing targets, these ones more violent than the Fearless Vampire Killers. A skinhead was lynched in Oregon. Someone mailed anthrax to the NRA.

"Crazy kids," Beach said to himself.

That was just the good news. The bad news was that President Pence also declared marshal law in San Francisco; dregs bused in from the South were now marching up and down the picturesque, undulating streets. War loomed with North Korea; cops killed more black people; the rich got richer and the poor got poorer: same shit, different day. Just out of curiosity, he flipped the channel over to Fox "News," which had decided to lead with a story about poor Hillary Clinton's emails. Beach laughed out loud and shut off the TV.

He then thought of Clare, jerked off, cleaned himself with a dirty sock beside the bed, and stared at the ceiling, hand cupping his balls, feeling sorry for himself. Were his testicles always so small? He resigned to ask his doctor tomorrow. He wondered whether he was broken. At forty-eight, he should have a wife, two kids, a stable work ethic, some sense of having accomplished something worth remembering. The Capitol attack was something, but he could never take credit for it. Where had he gone wrong?

Beach slept, momentarily forgot his heartache, irrevocably forgot his dreams, awoke the following day, showered, got dressed, and rode his bike to the doctor. There he was questioned, poked and prodded, and told he might have cirrhosis of the liver—a slow death sentence.

Things were looking up.

He called his ex-wife, went to the bank, withdrew the last hundred thousand dollars from his retirement account via two cashier's checks, and bicycled to a lawyerly restaurant near Super Court to meet the ever-vivacious Sarah Almeida, Esq.; his ex-wife of twenty years; law partner of five years; now an estranged, cynical friend. He ordered a glass of water, no straw—then changed his mind and ordered a martini.

Fuck the world.

He and Sarah had met in law school, dated insatiably, and married early. Their legal careers ascended concurrently. When she left Big Law and he left the D.C. Public Defender to form Almeida and Sands, P.C., they had been inseparable. Their practice flourished. They were the go-to defense attorneys for anyone charged with a street crime in D.C. But working together taxed their relationship in a way that domestic life had not. Their romance cooled considerably. Sometime before the bedbugs' black blood (try saying that three times fast), he discovered she was having an affair with her personal trainer, Roger Federer, no relation to the tennis player.

Initially enraged, Beach hired a private investigator named Phillip Nichols to get the evidence that would secure his upper hand in a swift divorce—but the more he discovered about his wife's infidelity, the more it turned him on. She stopped going to the gym altogether and spent most evenings at the same motel. Beach watched Phillip's videos of her coming and going. There was nothing inherently sexy about them, except that she arrived to the room in her work clothes and left in her gym clothes. When she came home she showered, and Beach imagined the things she must have done with Roger that night, the things she was trying to conceal from him. It made him crazy, he desired her more, and in a strange way it brought them closer together again, like they had been before Almeida and Sands.

But then Phillip got burned, and Beach confessed to Sarah about the surveillance, which had been ongoing for six months. They tried to reconcile, but passion again dwindled and distance grew. The bedbugs came, no doubt from one of Sarah's motel trysts with Roger. Traumatic insemination—a dick to the belly: their marriage, unable to sustain the distress, bled out.

"To what do I owe this invitation?" Sarah slipped into the seat across from him, hailed the server, and flitted her laughing, almond eyes from the center of Beach's stomach up to the top of his head. "You've lost some weight. Your eyes are yellow. You look like shit."

"You look as beautiful as ever," he said—and she did. Some new lines only accentuated her Brazilian bedroom eyes, which saw through him like a pane of glass.

The server appeared with Beach's drink. She asked for water. He upended the martini into his mouth and ordered another.

"Beach, what's wrong?" Her eyes were no longer laughing.

"I think I'm going to die, and I need you to do me a big favor."

"Oh, Beach. Is it the drinking?"

"Maybe. I'm waiting for some tests, but what I need now is actually a professional favor."

"Please tell me what's going on."

He told her what the doctor said. She began to cry. When his next drink came she swatted it off the table, apologized to the server, and stared at Beach sadly. "You are such a fucking idiot."

He removed one of the cashier's checks from his pocket and slid it across the table. It was made out to Sarah. "I want to retain you."

She glanced at the check, but didn't touch it. "Are you in trouble?"

"It's for a friend, a woman named Clare Swan."

"What, pray tell, would I be representing Ms. Swan *for?*" Recognition dawned on Sarah's face, and she laughed. "Wait! Isn't that your little legal assistant? Are you boinking her?"

"I'm serious, Sarah. You're the best defense attorney I know. I need you to do this for me, as a favor—the last favor I'll ever ask of you. I don't know if Clare will ever get in trouble or what the charges would be, but if it ever happens I need you to go to bat for her—for me."

Sarah put a finger on the check and slid it closer. "You need to give me more information. I can't agree to represent someone without knowing what she'll be charged with—without ever having spoken to her. And what if she's charged in a jurisdiction where I'm not barred? Depending on the charges, fifty thousand might not even be enough."

Beach put his hands on the table, palms up. "I will tell you that if there *are* any charges—and there might not be—they'll probably be filed in the Eastern District. You're barred in Virginia, so that's not a problem. And if fifty thousand's not enough, Clare's parents can afford the rest of your fees. Please Sarah, if I tell you any more you'll be a witness. I need you to trust me on this."

She folded the check and put it in her purse. "Okay, if she calls me I'll represent her—but only because I was such a bitch to you."

"You were never a bitch."

The server returned to clean up the glass and take their orders, and the talk turned to less controversial topics: Judge Swift's "definitive" ruling (by Beach's telling) that voting for Trump was inherently impeachable, Sarah's latest federal conspiracy trial (not guilty), her dog, and general Super Court gossip.

When they were done eating and hugged goodbye, he went to his office. Despite throwing away the burnt carpet and scrubbing the floor, the reception area still smelled like piss. He made himself a drink, then two more. He donned his cloak and ambled down to the National Mall, to the encampment now dubbed "Freedom City" by the Pence administration.

"The only thing worse than a bedbug is barefaced Orwellianism," he huffed.

Beach had avoided the area since returning from Dulles, but he had seen a feature about it on the news. Rows of modular buildings and round-topped dormitory tents connected with link tunnels were erected between the Washington Monument and the U.S. Capitol to house the occupying white shirts. There was a mess building, shower facilities, and even a large, dome-shaped chapel of the mega-church variety found in the South. The whole perimeter was cordoned off with gabion barriers—bullet proof, explosive proof—and manned by checkpoints. The thousand or so white shirts living inside the camp accompanied police on raids of suspected "alt-left terrorists and other agitators." They attacked protestors and anyone else they didn't like on a whim, with no accountability.

When he got to the Mall, he walked right up to the closest checkpoint. A white shirt with his trademark red hat and the word "deplorable" tattooed across his neck blocked the path. A nametag next to his tin badge read, "Travis S."

"Where do you think you're going?"

Beach smiled. "I'm a voracious liberal."

"A what?"

"You boys are doing fine work here at Freedom City. You got this town quite on edge."

Travis fidgeted with the hat's bill, clearly confused as to whether Beach was messing with him or not. "We, um, volunteered because we want to see America great again."

"You mean *white* again."

"You best get moving along."

"Under these pants I'm wearing women's underwear." Beach held his groin. "I'm queer as a three-dollar bill. I've been sucking cock since before you were a twinkle in your daddy's eye."

Travis chuckled and hefted his club onto his shoulder. "Get out of here, you crazy son-bitch—now—or I'm gonna bust your faggot head wide open."

Beach unfurled his cloak and spit straight in Travis' eye. "The only thing worse than a—"

It was dark when he woke up in the gutter on Constitution Avenue with his pockets turned out. Although his head felt like it had been inseminated by a dog-size bedbug, he never felt better—because he now had nothing left to lose.

14. Banned in D.C.

After returning to Woodland Terrace and resuming his monastic life for a few weeks, FD's eyes opened on a Tuesday morning and he immediately sensed that the world was irrevocably worse off than it had been the day before. He knocked on his grandmother's door—no response—and inside he found her, eyes closed, on her back, chest still. Nana, known by the D.C. government as Anita Hamdi, known by everyone else as "Grandma Hamdi," the kind, elderly, bespectacled woman, so known for her foul mouth, had passed quietly in her sleep. Her glasses sat on the nightstand beside the bed. FD kissed her cold cheek and wept.

He sat beside her in silence all morning until his stomach grumbled, and then he went into the kitchen, made coffee, and ate some cereal: generic cornflakes. Nana had given FD's father her sharp mind and her beautiful, inquisitive eyes. Her sense of humor, her great intelligence, and her cynicism had been responsible for making Bilal Hamdi who he was: FD's hero. She had also helped shape FD directly. His mother died from a heroin overdose when he was seven, and if not for some pictures he would barely remember her. But Nana had filled that maternal void, teaching him to respect women, even when they, like too many men, failed to live up to their potential.

When he was done with his cornflakes, he retrieved pens and spray paint from his room, pushed the kitchen table up against the refrigerator, opened the blinds, and stared at the kitchen's one blank, white wall. He had sketched his grandmother countless times in his life, ever since he was a little boy. He recalled how she looked now in the next room, relaxed in eternal repose. In a strange way, she looked younger. He remembered thinking the same thing about his father— how death changed him, even more than his time in the hospice, when he became emaciated, his face almost skeletal. When Bilal Hamdi finally succumbed to his fate, his eyes and mouth sank a bit. Not everyone would have noticed this, but to FD's eyes, it was as if he had become a different person, at peace with the world and with himself.

Using a hefty Sharpie Magnum (for this was a big canvas and the subject deserved a generous outline), he drew a squiggly line, her jawline, and connected it with a straight line: the bedspread. He paused to consider her ear and the wrinkles on her neck. He set the pen back on the table and switched to paint, always Krylon: gloss cinnamon for the shadows, copper cheeks, "metallic new penny" for the glints of refracted light. He pulled out the finer Sharpie Chisel to highlight the lines on her cheeks, the wrinkles on her bedspread, the edge of the nightstand, her glasses, and then he stopped.

"I miss Dad so much. I'll miss you too, Nana."

Most of his tears fell to the kitchen floor, but when he turned his head back to the painting after switching cans he flicked one tear onto the wall, where it landed between Nana's closed eyes and ran down the still-tacky paint on her face, leaving a noticeable trail. He wiped his eyes with the back of his hand. He thought of painting the wall white and starting over. Instead he dipped the tip of his pen into the tears that had collected on the linoleum floor, until there was a black puddle. He then used the tip as a quill to soak up the inky tears and draw the tangle of Nana's hair on the pillow. With a few flicks of the pen, he drew her eyelashes.

"You were never one to worry, Nana, but just in case you're worried now, I want you to know that no matter what happens I'm gonna be okay. My new friends are a little wild—but then, you know, so am I. So was Dad."

FD stopped to look at his finished painting. It was perfect, despite the line across her face left by his tear's trail. He blew softly on the ink and paint, so that it would set exactly where it was. He then picked up Nana's house phone and dialed 911 for the first time.

For a woman who was already dead, the emergency responders arrived faster than he expected. Within an hour he was standing out front, along with the entire neighborhood, as Nana, now covered with a sheet, was carted away on a gurney. His many "nephews" gave their condolences.

"Sorry, Uncle Ef-dee. Grandma Hamdi was like my Nana, too."

That afternoon there was an impromptu wake, as the community came together to remember Grandma Hamdi. Card tables and folding chairs were arranged in the courtyard. Solette and D'Andrea grilled chicken. Prophesy made potato salad. There were also burgers, mac and cheese, collard greens, candied yams, and chips. FD appreciated the gestures, even though his mind was somewhere else.

What happened at the hotel had left FD with an unsettled feeling about the Fearless Vampire Killers, not because he had not enjoyed fucking Clare (he had), or even tag-teaming her with Joe (he had seen and done wilder things), but because it changed his perception of Beach. Before, Beach had reminded him of his father, but now that association made FD uncomfortable. Although what they accomplished together on Capitol Hill had been amazing, the artistic/engineering feat of FD's lifetime, he was undecided whether he wanted to wage more war with them or not.

But whether or not the group reconvened after their agreed-upon respite, or FD chose to plan his next revolutionary act alone, doing nothing was no longer an option. The white shirts based in D.C. were now regularly menacing the African American neighborhoods, provoking fights and giving the "real" cops detailed to the ALT Task Force a reason to arrest people. Three of FD's nephews had succumbed to provocation, fought back, and were hauled off to the D.C. Jail, which was so full of so-called "suspected alt-left terrorists" and other resisters that a temporary correctional facility called the "Wild Camp" was erected on Kingman Island in the Anacostia River to house them all.

FD had just prepared his second plate of food when Junior Smalls, who so often took it upon himself to act as the block lookout, yelled, "Five-Oh!"

Everyone looked at each other and shrugged. It was early, and only a couple of the younger people were smoking weed. These people stepped inside. FD thought of going inside too, but he had a full plate of food and this was Nana's wake. He took a bite of potato salad and waited.

The white shirts rounded the corner with their clubs resting on their shoulders. One turned Junior's wheelchair over, dumping the boy onto the pavement. When his mother protested, she was smashed in the head, where she fell beside Junior. A woman screamed. There were about twenty-five of them, all wearing their signature white shirts, red hats, and khakis. They upended tables, kicked over the chairs, and dumped all of the food on the ground. FD sat perfectly still, even when a white shirt swatted the plate from his hand and raised his club, daring FD to do something.

"Langston Hamdi!" From around the corner marched Officer John Meyer, now sporting the new uniform of "sworn" officers (as opposed to the deputized volunteers) detailed to the ALT Task Force: gray, urban camouflage adorned with a tin badge.

Some of FD's nephews fought back, using the folding chairs as weapons. The courtyard erupted into a brawl. He thought of retrieving Officer Meyer's gun, which was still hidden in the wall behind his bed, but before he could do anything, two white shirts grabbed his arms and lifted him from the chair. FD willed himself to remain limp. If he resisted, they would surely arrest him, and there was nothing he could do if he were locked up in the Wild Camp.

"Take him into his grandma's house," Officer Meyer said, pushing FD's chest toward the backdoor.

"You can't come inside my home without a warrant."

"You know as good as I do, Mr. Hamdi, that you're not supposed to be living here. You can't refuse us entry, because it's not *your* house. Yesterday it was the residence of one Anita Hamdi, but today it's just a vacant public housing unit—which means it belongs to me."

They pushed him inside, cuffed his hands behind his back, and shoved him into a seat at the kitchen table. The white shirts ransacked the house. FD couldn't see what they were doing to the rest of the house, but in the kitchen they pulled all the boxes from the cupboards, dumped the rest of his cornflakes into the sink, and swiped all the food from the refrigerator onto the floor. Officer Meyer pulled up the second chair and sat beside him. One of the white shirts stood behind him, pressing his hands onto FD's shoulders.

Officer Meyer leaned across the table until his face was inches from FD's face. His breath smelled like cigarettes. "Want to tell me where Joseph Kaline is?"

"Who?"

"You know, your P.I. friend, the one who broke into my house to keep your sorry ass out of prison. The same one who was probably paid by George Soros to poison President Trump."

When FD laughed, the white shirt behind him slapped him hard on the head. "I don't know what you talking about. I wanna talk to my law—"

The man behind him grabbed his throat and squeezed. FD's airway closed, but he willed himself to remain still. It was only when he was about to pass out that Officer Meyer nodded and the grip relaxed. FD gasped for air.

Officer Meyer studied the painting of Nana on the wall. "That's really good." He then stood, upturned the table, and put his boot through the drywall, right in the middle of Nana's face.

FD closed his eyes and clenched his fists. "I wanna talk to my lawyer."

"Right, Beach Sands. We've got our eye on him too."

"Nothing," said a white shirt who appeared in the doorway.

Officer Meyer pointed his finger between FD's eyes. "You have twenty minutes to pack your shit and get the fuck out of here."

15. Joe Unleashed

A month after leaving to get ice, Joe awoke in the morning, boiled some water for coffee, stowed his tent, and shaved off his beard beside a stream. He washed his hair, put on the cleaner of his two shirts, and set off down the Catawba Mountain, planning to hike down to Blacksburg, Virginia for some long overdue human interaction.

After retrieving the cache they left near Chester Gap (in which he had also stowed his Uzi), he had hiked three hundred miles, averaging fifteen miles a day—but not straight along the Appalachian Trial. Although his feet generally carried him south, and he had a specific destination in mind—San Antonio, where he aimed to find his sister—he often veered down random trails. Sometimes he double-backed for no reason other than that he wanted to. Sometimes he continued down side trails for miles until he found another trail that wound back up the mountain in a different direction. He wandered into the Monongahela National Forest in West Virginia and spent a week in the George Washington and Jefferson National Forests. He never stopped except to sleep and buy more food when he needed it. With nothing but him and the great outdoors, and occasional hellos from passing through-hikers, he had had a lot of time to think.

Although his thoughts were as meandering as his footpath, they always returned to three topics: Geeta and Naagesh, the Fearless Vampire Killers, and Clare, specifically.

His Skype chats with Geeta had stopped being a weekly occurrence when he signed onto Civil War II, and now he had not spoken to her since before the Capitol siege. Naagesh was now three, and Joe was missing out on seeing his son walk and talk. Of course, Joe couldn't tell Geeta what he was doing; the NSA likely listened to those calls. He loved his family, and when he thought that his wife must now assume he abandoned her and Naagesh, it made him shudder in self-loathing. They had not seen each other in person in two years. He had been planning a trip to India to see them before he joined the Fearless Vampire Killers, but now—without knowing whether he was a wanted man or not—he could never show up at an airport. He wondered how he would ever see his family again.

Joe told himself he had made this great sacrifice—joining the Fearless Vampire Killers—because he wanted to make America a safer place for Geeta and Naagesh to return to, but in his heart he knew this was only part of the reason. Another part was his hatred for his father, and by extension all fascists. Joe reveled in teaching everyone how to make bombs and leading them on their first spate of attacks across the South. It was dharma that he should right his course in life and fight on the side of righteousness, and this felt good to him in the way that altruism always stokes the ego of the giver.

But it was difficult to see how his actions would benefit Geeta and Naagesh in the short term. As the show of force on the National Mall proved, the fascists had already won. He didn't truly believe there was anything in America worth salvaging.

So if America was already lost, and Joe recognized the selfishness of his hatred, why did he long to reunite with the Fearless Vampire Killers? Whenever his mind began to focus on the likely culprit, he tried to force it down another path, but like his roundabout trek to San Antonio he always returned to the same trail and the same conclusion: he was in love with Clare.

He couldn't get her out of his mind, and whenever he thought about their orgy in Dulles he seethed with jealousy. The first time he met Geeta she had been thirty feet up a rock face, and he had watched her rappel down, nimble and fearless, like she was born sideways. Although Clare was not a rock climber (that Joe knew of), there was a cool confidence in the way she handled herself, like the way she volunteered to light the first pipe bomb in Lynchburg. Joe loved that about her, even as he knew Clare was not right for him.

For one thing, she was quite obviously promiscuous and didn't seem to have the least interest in settling for Joe, or any other man. Poor Beach was doomed. Back when Joe was a skinhead, they had a name for women who hung out and slept around with different members of the crew: "boot buddies." Boot buddies were almost invariably obese, ugly, and dumb as a box of rocks. Funny, he thought—for all white supremacists' talk about their supposed genetic superiority, sexual selection didn't bode well for the so-called master race in the long run. Most of them couldn't afford to buy docile Eastern European brides.

Clare was nothing like a boot buddy. She was intelligent, fearless, funny, and gorgeous. Joe shook his head. They were cohorts in the war against fascism, he was already married to a wonderful woman, and he should stop letting his feelings cloud his judgment.

After a three-hour, downhill hike, he emerged into some semblance of civilization on the outskirts of Blacksburg, the home of Virginia Tech. He had not yet turned on the phone he picked up at the cache, and in Blacksburg he hoped to find a place to charge it and a Wi-Fi network so he could Skype with Geeta before it was too late in India. He just wanted to tell her that he was all right and that he was still hoping to make a trip to see her and Naagesh.

He walked past rural houses, gas stations, chain restaurants, and a few college dive bars before he found a diner that had free Wi-Fi.

A server appeared with a menu and led him to a booth with a plug. "You hiking the Appalachian Trial?" She had straight hair, her nose pierced, and a gap between her front teeth.

Joe sat down, nodded, and plugged in his phone. He had not spoken to another human in days.

"I want to do that someday. What can I get you to drink?"

Joe ordered coffee, asked for the Wi-Fi password, and switched on his phone.

Once connected, he scrolled through the news. President Pence had declared martial law in D.C., and white shirts now occupied the Mall in an encampment they were calling "Freedom City." What a joke. He was still chewing on that piece of news when his coffee arrived. The phone then chose that moment to update. Joe waited and sipped his coffee.

Update completed, he had to restart the phone, and then his pancakes arrived. He ate half his food as quickly as he could, downloaded Skype, set up a new account, put in his earphones, and typed in her ID from memory. It was already ten o'clock at night in India. She didn't answer. He ate the rest of his pancakes. After subsisting largely on beans and bread, the pancakes were the best things he had eaten all month. Geeta called him back as he was savoring his last bite.

When her face crystalized, Joe's path became clear again. He wiped some syrup from his chin and smiled broadly. "Hello, Janu!"

Her mouth was open, her forehead pinched. "Joe, they came here looking for you."

"They? Who's they?"

"I don't know. The FBI? Some terrorism task force? There were two men. They asked where you were. I told them I didn't know."

The server came and filled Joe's coffee. He waited until she returned to the counter. "They asked for me by name?"

"They said you blew up some statue."

"Motherfuck…"

He struggled to think. He had been out of touch with the world for a month. Had they also identified the others? Could they all be in jail already? Maybe he was the last one who had not been caught. Probably not: they had been so careful. FD's minivan was not traceable back to them. There was nothing that could tie them to the explosives or the trebuchet. They had meticulously wiped off and burned everything, and they had used gloves and even Tyvek suits. Obviously Officer Meyer suspected him or he wouldn't have put the GPS tracker under his car, but he had no proof—certainly not enough proof to send two agents to India to harass his wife.

Wait, why had they told Geeta about the statue?

He looked at the fork in his hand, where he had singed himself with the plasma cutter. There was a circular scar there now. He had seen a drop of blood fall onto the statue's base. They had blown up the statue, but was it possible they could have found the blood anyway? They had his DNA on file from his arrest in Atlanta.

"Those people are crazy, Joe. You need to get out of America while you can."

"Hold on," he said. "What did they tell you, exactly?"

At his urging, she described two Americans, one who mentioned living in India—perhaps State Department Diplomatic Security—and another who had a southern accent and belonged to some anti-terrorist task force in America. They had threatened to extradite Geeta and have her locked up in America for harboring a fugitive. Her parents kicked them out.

"Why did they think I was there?" Joe said, although he was already working out the answer before the words left his lips.

Since they knew who he was, they could pull his marriage certificate. It wouldn't have taken them long to find where Geeta's permanent residency application had been denied. It had her address in India. They had likely searched his home already. His car was still in the Dulles parking lot, or it had been towed away by now. They might have found the phone he put in the guy's bag. He had only paid cash for food since leaving the hotel. There would be no trace of him left in the United States. It would be natural to assume he might have left the country somehow and made his way to India.

He looked at the phone in his hand. Now that he had called Geeta they would know this phone belonged to him, and they would trace it. They would know exactly where he was. They could be eavesdropping on this call, assuming he would eventually contact his wife. The bottom line was that he needed to get out of there—quick.

"Listen to me very carefully, Geeta. I have to go now, but I will come to India as soon as I can. I'm sorry that I've caused trouble for you and your family. Please kiss Naagesh on the forehead for me. I love you. Good bye."

"Oh Joe, I love you too! Please be careful!"

He ended the call, asked for the check, paid cash, and went to the restroom. There he took the Uzi from his pack and wedged it in his belt beneath his shirt. It felt conspicuous, but after inspecting himself in the mirror he decided it was sufficiently hidden to the casual observer. He wished he had had time to crap at the diner, but they could already be on the way to arrest him by now. He left the diner, tucked the phone—power on, alerts silenced—beneath the bumper of a parked car, and headed straight back to the mountain.

The phone signal might throw them off for a bit, or the police might go straight to the diner and show his picture to the server, who would tell them he had just left and was hiking the Appalachian Trail.

As he was walking along a rural road, thinking through his plans, a Blacksburg Police car shot past him. Break lights flashed. The car pulled over two hundred feet in front of him. Joe winced, but he kept walking. When he was about fifty feet away, the officer heaved his massive belly out of the car and watched Joe approach, scowling, hat pulled low, legs slightly apart, hand on his gun. Joe smiled, took several more steps, and then yanked the Uzi from his belt.

The cop dropped to one knee, pulled out his pistol and just about emptied his magazine in Joe's direction. At that range, if the cop hit him with his handgun it would have just been dumb luck. The Uzi held three times as many bullets and had a longer barrel: the advantage was Joe's.

He dove to the ground and lay as flat as it is humanly possible to lie flat on the ground. He wiggled forward like a worm about ten more feet. The cop reloaded and kept shooting. Bullets landed in the gravel all around Joe's body. A few of them were pretty close, but they were not closely grouped.

When he was near enough that he thought he could make the shot, he aimed carefully and fired repeatedly, taking his time, holding his breath, until he pinned the cop behind the car and shot out one of the rear tires. He watched the rear of the car sink to one corner.

He then stood and ran into the woods. There was no way that fat fucker could keep up with him there, and without a car he also couldn't drive ahead and cut Joe off.

Of course, it would be hard to outrun the police radio.

Joe dashed through a patch of woods and came out on a field with several young bulls. The Catawba Mountain showed in the distance—freedom—but it was a long way. He hoped the Blacksburg Police Department didn't have a helicopter. He crawled under an electric fence, jogged through the field, and caught his breath momentarily behind a barn. He looked at his magazine: only twelve rounds left. He slammed the clip back in the gun. When he peaked around the side he saw two cops, one with a German shepherd, walking the perimeter of the electric fence. They were on Joe's trail. He continued jogging toward the mountain, trying to keep the barn between him and the cops. He heard yelling in the distance. They had spotted him.

He ran up a hill, scurried under another fence, passed a gravel road, and darted into a patch of woods. A cop car skidded to a stop on the gravel road right behind him. He kept running. He heard more shouting and a gunshot. It was loud—a rifle: the cops now had a decided advantage in a gunfight. His only hope was to lose them.

There was no trail here. The ground was overgrown. He leaped over thickets and brambles, and jogged left and then right around trees. The one thing going for him was that he was in excellent shape. These cops had ceased being in good shape many donuts ago.

But the dog, denied donuts, was in stellar condition—an animal that existed for no other purpose than to hunt men like Joe.

He stumbled upon a stream leading down the mountain, and he jogged straight up the bank, leaping from rock to rock. As little vegetation grew near the bank, it was as good as a trail. He thought he had made some distance, but then the dog barked behind him. It was close. He turned and saw its white teeth gnashing. It leapt straight for him. He shit his pants as its teeth closed around his ankle.

16. Tinker Mountain Manhunt

A face flashed on the gym's TV, and the treadmill on which Clare's legs bounded in place, set at a speedy 7.5, pitched her straight onto the floor. She tumbled backwards, hit her head against the machine behind her, and rolled onto her side. The gym-goer on the adjacent treadmill rushed to help, but Clare leapt up, waved the woman off, and looked up at the screen. There he was—Joseph Kaline, smiling, shock of red mane: wanted for terrorism.

The government knew who he was. The picture they showed looked like his driver's license photo, or maybe his private detective ID. Did this mean they were also looking for Beach? FD? Did they know Clare's identity too? With no sound, she couldn't tell what was happening.

The headline simply read: "Manhunt in Blacksburg."

She realized she was gawking at the screen. The woman who had offered to help her was watching her curiously. Deciding she had already drawn enough attention to herself, Clare forced a casual smile, walked briskly to the locker room, snatched her messenger bag from the locker, bolted from the gym, hopped on her bike, and pedaled home as fast as her legs could propel her—which was pretty damn fast.

After two weeks in Berlin and another two back in D.C., studying for the bar, laying low, working out, new haircut, weed intake halved, she was now back in top physical and mental shape—not withstanding, respectively, her tooth, still missing, and the looming Nazi menace. Physically, she immersed herself in yoga, spinning, swimming, and weights. She was eating more leafy greens and less dairy. Her body was chiseled like a sentient arrowhead.

Mentally, she had come to terms with her self-destructiveness and had begun to understand its origins. Reared in Vermont's pristine, blue bubble, she understood the world as governed by reasonable and fundamentally good people, despite ideological differences. When she had witnessed evidence of America's fundamental rottenness and stupidity on TV (case in point: Duck Dynasty), she assumed, like many Americans, that it was solely for entertainment purposes. Such idiocy must be a Hollywood fantasy, intended solely to induce laughter and ridicule. Such vapidity must be satire, created to help "real Americans" appreciate the values that actually matter: compassion, empathy, and love.

Her cousin's malevolent smile put a crack in her simulacrum: some Americans, even ones who had theretofore been dear to her, were in fact rotten. But the twelve-year-old Clare had glossed over this lesson and stitched her bubble back together with counseling and Band-Aids. Through high school, college, and law school she met plenty of people who did bad things, but never did she write them off as "bad people"; they were merely people whose situations caused them to make bad choices. Then, nearly a third of the population voted for Donald J. Trump—a demonstrable crook, racist, sociopath—and it was no longer possible for her to ignore the world's evil. Her worldview imploded under the crushing force of America's profound sickness.

But she had come to terms with this now. She had just needed some time to readjust to her new understanding of the world. During her month away from the Fearless Vampire Killers, she reburied Joshua's memory. Although she hadn't spoken to Beach since the hotel, he was back again on her list of favorite people. He might be stubbornly unreasonable, eccentric, mad, and unabashedly horny—but he had a good heart, which is what mattered most.

She had been looking forward to their scheduled reunion, still two weeks away, and the resumption of their activities: particularly the violent ones. She missed the boys: Joe, so sweet, troubled, but fundamentally good; and FD, sad, beautiful, and extraordinarily gifted. She had no regrets, either for the war they waged or for the fun night they shared on the eve of the Capitol siege. If enjoying sex made Clare a whore, then she would just be a whore, along with every other man, woman, and animal on earth—from the spare arctic hare to the zaftig zebra. Fuck her Aunt Becky and all judgmental shrews forever. Had Clare hurt anyone? Hardly: hearts are resilient. She knew their friendship would recover once they returned to fomenting war.

But the fact that the ALT Task Force had identified Joe and were now hunting him in the wilderness changed everything.

She locked her bike outside her apartment, bounded upstairs, switched on the news (volume up), showered, and packed a backpack with abundant food and all her camping gear. She then donned the pack and huffed the two miles to Beach's house. Her plan: rouse him from whatever state of drunkenness she found him in, find FD, who could procure another untraceable vehicle, and together head to Blacksburg to rescue Joe from the government's clutches.

However, when she knocked on the door it was FD who answered, grinning, shoeless, shirtless, his well-developed pecs spanning the entire doorway.

She threw her arms around him. "Fuck, it's good to see you again."

He lifted her off the ground and pulled her inside, kicking the door closed with his heel.

"If you had a beret you'd look just like Patty Hearst." Beach lay propped up on the living room couch, his feet resting on several pillows. He wore camouflage shorts and a mismatched flannel shirt. "I'd offer you a drink, but we were just heading out the door."

"Patty Hearst didn't have bangs." Clare let go of FD and dropped her pack next to two others perched against the wall near the front door, beneath a new mural of an elderly black woman, kind, bespectacled.

Beach smiled broadly, pulled himself from the couch, and limped over to Clare. He seemed unstable, but his arms were strong as they embraced her. "I missed you so much," he said.

She buried her face against his chest. "Oh Beach, are you okay? I'm sorry about leaving you at the hotel. I just needed some time to think."

"That's okay, my dear. I'm fine." He kissed her forehead and let her go. "My legs have just been a tad swollen lately, but Ef-dee's been taking good care of me."

FD pulled on a black t-shirt. "We should probably get moving. Joe's out there all alone."

After the tearful reunion, they walked three blocks to FD's "borrowed," mauve Chevy Uplander, shut off their cell phones, and took turns driving to Roanoke. As they drove, they caught each other up on their last month's doings. FD's grandmother had died, and Officer Meyer had kicked him out of his home in Woodland Terrace. He subsequently moved in with Beach, which seemed to suit both of them just fine. Beach had tentatively resumed his defense practice, purveying justice through legal channels. In lieu of rent, FD had adorned his house with a half-dozen murals. She told them about

Berlin, dropping acid at the Berghain nightclub, and about her daytrip to Wittenberg, where Martin Luther nailed his famous "95 Theses," which kicked off the Reformation.

"There aren't enough 'fuck you' notes nailed to doors anymore," Beach said, whipping their minivan onto I-81 southbound. "If every stinking millennial with parents who supported Trump were to nail a 'fuck you' note to mommy and daddy's door there'd be no need for a civil war. The baby boomers would all wither and die—and we'd all be better off." A few minutes passed, and he asked: "Do evangelicals take the Eucharist at church?"

FD shrugged. "No fucking clue."

Clare pressed her tongue where her lateral incisor had once been. "Why?"

"Just curious."

When talking grew tiresome, they turned on the radio, hoping for news about Joe. Although many stations talked about the manhunt currently underway for the "heavily armed terrorist," there was very little *new* news—and much of it was contradictory. During their five-hour drive, the ALT-Task Force had cordoned off a five-hundred-square-mile section of wilderness around part of the Appalachian Trail; detained a suspect who used the pseudonym "Percy Fletcher"; determined Mr. Fletcher was not the man they were looking for; detained another suspect, male, unnamed (no more word on him yet); charged Mr. Fletcher for making illegal moonshine; crashed a helicopter (miraculously, nobody injured); and killed another suspect, male, name also withheld.

Nobody in the Uplander asked the obvious question: was Joe already dead? Clare thought of him alone in the woods, chased like an animal, and she pushed the gas pedal down a little harder.

Meanwhile, according to the news, there had been other leftist attacks throughout the country. An evangelical church of the rightwing extremist variety was firebombed in Alabama (nobody injured). A white shirt was beaten into a coma in California. An old man caught on video giving a racist rant at a Wal-Mart was accosted in the parking lot, doused in canola oil, and sprinkled with confetti. Stanley Congdon, the Task Force czar, was claiming that all of these things were part of one unified "alt-left terrorist" group, which was somehow linked to the conspiracy theory around President Trump's death. George Soros and Hillary Clinton were wanted for questioning.

"We—meaning the Fearless Vampire Killers—agreed not to hurt anyone," Beach said, "but does anyone feel guilty about the white shirt?"

They rode on in silence.

Clare was still at the wheel when they passed their first roadblock on Route 311, just outside the Roanoke city limits. It consisted of a single Virginia State Trooper with a wide-brimmed hat who was stopping every eastbound vehicle. As their Uplander was traveling westbound, however, they flew past, unencumbered. The road grew steeper. They lost their radio signal as they gained elevation. FD twisted the dial to find another station with more news, while Beach, in the backseat, studied the map.

Without cell phones they had no way to communicate with Joe, but he was reportedly last seen near Blacksburg, about forty miles south. Before they blew up the truck in Lynchburg, Joe had them hide a cache somewhere near a place called Tinker Mountain. Using a code, he had given everyone the coordinates, which Beach had used to put an "x" on their topographical map. Their only hope was that Joe, trapped in the woods, hungry, alone, would come for the cache. They could then sneak him past the roadblocks. It was a lot to hope for.

When they were within a few miles of the trailhead, Clare pulled the minivan down a dirt road, behind a dilapidated barn. They hauled out their packs, and using a compass hiked, as the terrain allowed, due northwest. Beach got winded every hundred yards or so, but it was a cool day, and the woods were pleasant. A helicopter passed by when they had hiked about a mile. They all hugged the nearest tree and remained still. The chopper passed. They trekked on. They got to the stream just as it grew dark, and there they rested for the fortieth time, ate some sandwiches Clare had made, and filled their purifier from the stream.

She pressed the water through the filter and poured it into her canteen. "Is any of this starting to look familiar?"

FD shook his head. "Not yet, but last time we were on the trail."

Beach sat against a tree, stared at the map, and scratched his beet-red forehead. "I *think* we're close."

Rested and fed, they followed the creek up the mountainside as the sky grew dark, until they came to a moonlit pond. Here the creek babbled louder, and the wind whistled through the pines. She gazed across the pond for any sign of another person, but the edges of the pond were shrouded in shadows and the water rippled uniformly.

FD gestured across the pond and whispered, "It's over there."

They skirted the water's edge, staying well in the shadows, their footfalls muffled by pine needles. They forded another creek, scrambled silently up a cliff face, and slid down into a dry creek bed. Here was a rock as big as a mobile home on one side of the rift. FD flickered his flashlight onto the rock's face, illuminating a small portrait of his father etched into the granite. They were very close.

He led them further up the creek, to a second large rock, and here they edged their way to the other side, where the rock was wedged against the mountain. The hollow between the rock and the mountain formed a triangular cave filled with a dead shrub. FD moved the shrub (already detached at the roots) and shone his flashlight inside.

"It's still there, untouched." He switched off the light.

They stood in the darkness, silent for some time.

"No, this is good," Beach finally said. "If he's still out there, and he comes for the cache, we can be here waiting for him. We just need to be far enough away from it that if we're stopped we can disavow any knowledge of what's inside there."

"What exactly *is* in the cache?" she asked.

FD started back down to the creek. "Actually, we don't know. Joe packed it. Definitely food, cash, a burner phone, a water purifier... But what else? Maybe a gun or two? You know Joe."

"Do you think he packed any gin?"

She put the shrub back at the cave's opening and followed after them. "We need clear heads tonight."

"My head has never been clearer."

They backtracked around the pond some distance and then climbed up the mountain, taking a different route, until they found a relatively flat spot to pitch a tent. They were far enough from the cache that they might credibly disavow all knowledge of it, whatever was inside: just a motley trio of backpackers spending a peaceful night beside a pond.

Tent pitched, air mattresses inflated, Clare said, "I'll take the first shift to keep an eye on the cache."

Beach shook his head. "Let's play rock-paper-scissors for the first shift."

First game: Clare and Beach both chose scissors, and FD paper.

FD started back to the pond, but Clare put a hand on his shoulder. "I'm sorry, but in a three-way game of rock-paper-scissors the odd symbol is *only* a winner when it beats the other two."

"Clare's right."

"Fucking lawyers."

Next game: all rocks. After two more games, Beach won. Another game determined that Clare would get second shift and FD the third.

After Beach lumbered into the shadows, she retired to the tent, followed by FD. It had been an exceedingly long day. Since falling off the treadmill that morning they had driven five hours and hiked at least ten miles. The ground beneath her sleeping bag was rocky, and the air mattress did little to help.

She lay on her back, staring up at the green nylon. "This stress is killing me, not knowing if Joe's alive. I don't see how I'm gonna sleep tonight."

"You want some dick? That might help you sleep."

She laughed. "That's a generous offer, Ef-dee—but if Beach can forgo gin for one night I think I can get by without dick. Besides, that mop on your head that you try to pass off for hair smells a bit… ripe."

He grunted.

She turned toward him, moving her body off a rock that was digging into her ribs. "Do you know why Beach is complaining about his legs?"

"He doesn't talk about it. A couple days ago he could barely walk to the store. To be honest, I was surprised he kept up with us today."

"He's nothing if not determined." She sighed and put her hand on his chest. "On second thought, I'll take you up on your offer, but only because I want to put you between me and these fucking rocks."

"Sure thing."

Sleeping bags unzipped, clothing sufficiently loosened, she sucked his dick until it was hard and then straddled him. She guided him inside her, brushing past her clit, nearly bumping against her cervix. She sucked his tongue. Cushioned from the relentless stones, worries gone (for the moment), she rocked her pelvis into him until her world exploded in a dizzying translucent-green haze.

Awash with oxytocin endorphins, she pulled on her jeans and retreated to her own sleeping bag. He was snoring within five minutes, and she was not far behind. Her sleep, however, was fitful and dreamless, beset by rocks and worries about Joe and Beach. She awoke as FD traced his finger along her jawbone.

"I can take the next shift if you want. I'm up anyway."

She smiled and stretched. "No, I'll do it. I want to."

Just then there was rustling outside. She froze. FD reached for his flashlight. Dry leaves crackled. Then the tent flap unzipped all at once as if by a ghost, and in popped a haggard face—bald and white like the moon.

"Here's Johnny!"

Clare kicked the face square in its chin before realizing it was Joe. "You scared the crap out of us, asshole! We thought you might be dead!"

"Look whom I found rooting around the cache," Beach said from outside the tent. "He wanted to surprise you."

She and FD each grabbed one of Joe's arms and pulled him inside, where they embraced him and rolled around until they almost broke the tent.

"Easy on the ankle," Joe said.

"What the fuck happened?" Clare held her nose. "You smell like shit."

Joe propped himself on his elbows. "It's a long story, which you'll hear when we have more time—but I have to tell you, these ALT Task Force folks know my name, and they're crawling all over this mountain right now. We need to get moving—quick."

"Oh, Joe!" she said. "Where can we go? They're going to chase you forever."

"I've been thinking about that a lot. In all the movies I've ever seen where someone's running from the law they always go to Mexico. I'm thinking that if I can get to there, I can find my way to India, to be with Geeta again."

Beach's head appeared between the tent flaps. "We better get moving. Mexico's a long way from Tinker Mountain."

Joe kissed Clare squarely on the lips, planted one on FD's cheek for symmetry's sake, and shimmied from the tent. "But I ain't going *nowhere* until we chase those motherfucking white shirts out of D.C."

17. Strategic Dilemmas

Testicles shrunken to the size of marbles, shaking slightly, sweating profusely, Beach laid in the dirt with his head on Clare's lap, his swollen feet propped on a rock. Above him, just beyond the lovely curvature of Clare's jawline, the stars danced in the moonless sky. Although it was cool, the mosquitos were relentless. He had largely given up trying to swat them, for he was too slow. Instead he imagined that every mosquito that pricked his skin was electrocuted, as if by a bug zapper. Forces beyond his control were at play; he resigned himself to their blood sucking, because every one that fried itself on his high-voltage skin became a new star. He may be eaten alive, but the universe would remain—beautiful, incandescent, mysterious, and hopeful.

He said to the others gathered around the fire: "In the spirit of overt honesty, I know we agreed on only targeting things—not people—but my position may have evolved."

"You mean devolved." Clare's lovely jawline straightened out, lips descended from the sky and planted a kiss on his forehead. (Maybe there is a God, he thought.) "We're *not* killing anyone," she said. "What other revolutionaries do is their own business."

After sneaking Joe past the checkpoint in Roanoke, they had driven due east, sideways across Virginia, until they reached Pocahontas State Park, just south of Richmond. There they used a fake ID and paid cash for a campsite of the car-camping variety. Trees were altogether sparse, outnumbered by their neighbors' RVs and popup trailers. Smell of charcoal, hotdogs, and pine needles; campfires glowed; and a radio somewhere was playing a Taylor Swift song.

"I agree with Beach," Joe said, ankle swathed in bandages, his face enshrouded in the shadow cast by his hoody. "How can we get the fascists off the Mall without hurting any of them?"

Beach turned his head toward the fire. "If we're going to beat fascism, we may *have to* hurt people, even kill them—because fascism is an ideology. We can destroy their monuments. We could even find a way to run them off the Mall. But the evil will live on inside people's minds—because fascist minds are intractable to reason."

"Sociopaths," Clare whispered.

"If there's anything worse than a bedbug..."

FD blew out a flaming marshmallow on his stick. "That's just it. They're immoral. We're not. They kill and hurt people, and then just lie about it—and they get away with it over and over again: Michael Brown, Freddie Gray, Philando Castile—"

"Sandra Bland, Heather Heyer." Clare took a drag from her vape pen.

"Lady Liberty, Lady Justice, Prudentia..." Beach swatted at a mosquito on his wrist, missed, and pulled himself reluctantly from Clare's lap.

Joe tossed another log on the fire. "They collude with authoritarians to rig elections and kill with impunity, so why shouldn't we strike back? They're never going to change."

"You sure about that, Joe?" Beach sat up, cross-legged beside Clare, palms toward the fire. "I think we should approach this like rational people—lay out our goals, our resources, and then we can discuss our options." He extended his right hand to Clare and his left hand to FD. They then held Joe's hands, forming a circle around the fire. All heads turned to Beach, who asked, "What do you all want most?"

Joe spoke first: "Another thrombotic stroke."

"I'm afraid that's strictly between Pence and his imaginary friend."

"Well, then how about building a cannon and blasting the white shirts off the Mall?" Joe said.

"But then we're attacking people and not things," Clare said. "What I'd like most is to attack them with irony and truth, to expose them for the bigoted, morally vapid hypocrites they are. If we try to physically hurt them, then we're no better than they are." She looked across the fire. "What do you want, Ef-dee?"

"I wanna make something beautiful that will inspire others to take a stand and fight back."

Beach nodded. "Okay, so what are our resources?"

"Without my tools and a place to work, we probably can't make bombs again."

"Okay, no bombs," Beach said. "Isn't there any P.I. stuff you could do?"

"I doubt I still have access to any investigative databases. Otherwise we could possibly find Stanley Congdon's home address. I suppose I could ask Phillip to help us out…"

"Phillip Nichols?"

"You know him?"

"He owes me a favor."

Clare's eyes fixated on the fire, and she said quietly, "There's always Garth Simonson."

"Garth who?" Joe asked.

"It's just some guy Beach and I know who works for the government. He might be susceptible to blackmail or something."

"Okay," Joe said. "Say that we could get inside Freedom City. What could we do inside that would inspire others to fight back, if that's our goal?"

The vape pen made a round, and even Beach—who positively ached for a drink—took a long hit. "We could vasectomize all the white shirts in their sleep."

"We could tear gas them back across the Potomac," Joe said. "Or mustard gas…"

FD shook his head. "No carcinogens."

"Why can't we just burn their tents down?" Clare asked.

"Not without hurting or killing anyone," Joe said. "Anyway, those things are probably made of fire-resistant materials."

Beach swatted at a mosquito on his hand, missed again. "We'd need an army to do any of that stuff without hurting anyone. There are about a thousand white shirts inside Freedom City, and attacking the White House would basically be impossible."

"Well, not impossible…" FD said. "It sounds like what we need are numbers."

"But if we try to recruit more people, we'll expose ourselves," Clare said.

"I'm already exposed," Joe said.

"And I don't care." Beach released his comrades' hands and used FD's shoulder to stand.

FD helped him up. "The problem is you're both the wrong color, and Joe has that awful southern accent. The people we'd need aren't gonna trust either of you enough to stick their necks out, unless they know who you are."

"Wait a second!" Clare shot up like a spring. "The white shirts are running around the city harassing specific people, right? What if we could get their list of 'alt-left terrorist' suspects and approach those people ourselves? We know from the other attacks there are others out there, just like us. If we banded together with them, we'd have an army."

"Would your buddy Garth actually give us that kind of information?"

"He's *not* my buddy—but he might be persuaded."

Beach put an arm around Clare. "It sounds like we may have ourselves the beginning of another grand plan." He released her and staggered toward the van. "I'm going to go buy some bug spray."

"Wait, I have some." Clare moved toward the tents.

"No, not that natural shit. It doesn't work. I want something with DEET—and gin."

Clare sighed. "Wait, I'll go with you."

As they climbed into the van, Clare in the driver's seat, Joe muttered to FD, "Weird, I don't think I've been bitten once..."

They had rolled quietly past the showers, trash bins, and the campsite office, when Clare abruptly stopped the van, killed the engine, and turned to him. "Beach, what's going on with you? You haven't been yourself lately. What's wrong?"

"We're all bound by our facticity." He reached into his pocket and pulled out his ex-wife's business card, which he set in her hand. "If the enemy catches us, call the attorney on that card. I paid her retainer for you, so she already represents you."

Clare squinted at the card in the dark. "Sarah Almeida? Isn't that your ex-wife? What did you tell her?"

"I didn't tell her anything. She's a better lawyer than I ever was. She'll help you if I can't."

Clare nodded silently, tucked the card in her shirt pocket, and turned the key. The Uplander grumbled back to life. "You realize there's no way I'm letting you buy liquor, right?"

"You can't stop me. I'm a grown-ass man."

"That's debatable."

"I love you."

"I love you too." She turned onto the main road, toward the closest supermarket. "But no liquor."

18. "Uncle Ef-dee"

"Isn't it some shit that if you shoot a K-9 that's trying to bite your ass you can be tried for murder, as if the dog's an actual person?" Boom, one of FD's many "nephews," opened the breech of his shotgun and snapped it shut again with a menacing click; he had been doing this over and over again for an hour. The gun, double-barreled, sawed off to the length of a baby's arm, was tucked between his knees, pointed at the passenger floorboard. "Yet, cops can kill black people like we're fucking dogs?"

"They just mad you shooting their property," said Phat Rat, FD's "niece," who was in the driver's seat. "Back when niggas was their property, they got real upset about that too." She was slunk low, the ski mask's eyeholes pulled over her eyes, but not her mouth, so that she looked something like a black Batwoman.

"Preach," Boom said.

Alone in the backseat, FD kept his eyes on the little dot on his phone that indicated Garth Simonson's whereabouts. "Honestly, I think my man felt bad about the dog."

The breech clicked again. "Shit, they the ones trained the dog to attack people."

Despite having known these two kids since they were born, FD didn't know their real names—and he didn't want to. To them, he was simply "Uncle Ef-dee." In Woodland Terrace, only snitches ask personal questions, and there were no snitches in this car. FD knew Boom was one of D'Andrea's sister's half-brothers, but he couldn't recall how he met Phat Rat, who came from Barry Farms. They were among those in the neighborhood dealt less than a full deck—educated at a public school whose scant resources were funneled to more affluent charter schools, woefully unprepared for anything but manual labor, blocked from making a livable wage, and perpetually tempted by the "salvation" of drugs and violence. The products of a systemically racist society, unchecked they'd likely be killed or imprisoned before they turned twenty-five. But all that mattered tonight was that they were discrete, reasonably smart, and mildly psychopathic—perfect additions to the Fearless Vampire Killers, even if they hadn't yet been officially inducted.

It was a Saturday night, and they were gathered in a "borrowed," black Chevy Impala—gloved and clad in black—pulled over on the side of the road in a wooded area just a few blocks from Garth's house in Herndon, Virginia. It was a providentially quiet neighborhood. Joe had gotten a GPS tracker from another private detective, who had also looked up Garth's home address for them. Meanwhile, Clare had made a date with Garth, who would be leaving any minute to meet her at a restaurant in Tyson's Corner.

FD was still unclear how Clare and Beach knew someone who worked for the White House under Stanley Congdon, the czar of the ALT Task Force, but like his nieces' and nephews' real names and Joe's encyclopedic knowledge of explosives, FD figured it was their own business. Only snitches worry too much about personal details. What was important was that Garth might give them information they could use to rid D.C. of Freedom City.

The blinking light moved. "Here we go."

As Boom and Phat Rat pulled on their ski masks, FD snatched a heavy cloth bag from the backseat floorboard, bolted from the car, and sprinted fifty feet in the direction of Garth's house. He dumped the caltrops on the asphalt and kicked a clump of the spikey, tire-puncturing devices to spread them out evenly on the road's surface. He then ran back to the car. Headlights rounded the corner. He crouched behind the Impala and pulled on his mask. Headlights got brighter, engine louder. He hunkered low. Then tires exploded, sparks flew, brake lights flashed—and Garth's red Ford Mustang skidded to the side of the road directly behind the Impala.

His niece and nephew sprang from the car, guns trained on the Mustang. Garth slammed the car in reverse. Phat Rat drove the barrel of her Beretta 9mm though the window, reached into the car, and pulled Garth out by his collar. She was half the man's size, but she was strong.

"Please don't kill me! You can have my car!"

Phat Rat smacked him on the head with her barrel. "Shut the fuck up, bitch. Ain't nobody want your crappy car."

They dragged him behind the Impala. Boom frisked him, taking his cell phone and a small handgun. He shut the cell phone off and stuck the gun in his pocket. Phat Rat moved the Mustang further off the road, returning with Garth's travel bag. FD pulled a sleeping bag from the Impala's trunk, spread it on the ground, and unzipped it.

Boom ordered Garth to lay down flat inside. They then zipped Garth up in the bag, which they secured with ratchet tie-downs, until he was rolled up like a big fascist burrito.

As Garth's head was still poking out, Phat Rat put a racquetball in his mouth and taped it shut with a piece of duct tape. Over his head she slipped a canvas grocery bag—perforated with holes near the mouth—and tied it loosely around his neck with a drawstring. Only then did they remove their masks. Boom and Phat Rat tossed their captive in the trunk while FD went back to collect the caltrops that were still on the road. When he returned to the Impala, Phat Rat twisted the ignition key and the Impala shot out of Garth's neighborhood.

FD's fingers shook as he sent a one-word group text to Joe and Beach's burner phones: "Bagged."

Clare was at that moment offline, waiting at the restaurant, making sure to be clearly "seen" by various video cameras. She would dutifully wait for Garth for an hour, sending him occasional texts from her regular cell phone, asking when he would get there, just to keep up the pretense that she wasn't involved in his kidnapping. After an hour, she would reconvene with Beach. Meanwhile, Beach and Joe were standing by in D.C., prepared to exploit whatever information FD and his cousins could get from Garth.

Phat Rat drove them away from Tyson's Corner, across Northern Virginia, to a decrepit motel along Route 1. There they carried Garth into a ground-floor room and tossed him on the bed, which they had already covered with a plastic drop cloth. They put their masks back on, and FD undid Garth's hood. He was sobbing and drenched in sweat, his eyes nearly as wide as the ball in his mouth. FD ripped off the tape and let him spit out the slippery racquetball, which stuck to the plastic beside the sleeping bag.

Garth gasped for air, square jaw quivering. "You can have whatever you want! Please don't hurt me! I have a wife and three kid—"

Boom put the shotgun barrels between his eyes. "If you don't shut the fuck up right now I'm gonna blow your motherfucking head off. You understand?"

Garth stared cross-eyed at the barrels and nodded slowly. When Boom removed the gun there were two red rings impressed on his forehead, like the fake "eyes" on a butterfly's wings.

Although outwardly he maintained a mask of calmness, FD inwardly recoiled at his nephew's viciousness. He had to remind himself that Garth was the leader of the white shirts in Freedom City, responsible for untold violence. FD had personally watched these fascists assault his nephews in the courtyard, before he was evicted from his childhood home. One had knocked Beach unconscious and left him in the gutter. They had even smashed out Clare's tooth and probably cracked her rib.

He gritted his teeth and dumped the contents of Garth's bag onto the bed: white shirt uniform, tin badge, ID card, electric toothbrush, deodorant, a phone charger, a box of condoms, a bottle of Pyrat Cask rum, and a personal laptop.

He put everything but the laptop back inside the bag and then flipped open the laptop's screen. He sat on the chair beside the bed. "What's the password?"

"Honestly, that's not even my comp—"

Boom stuck the shotgun in Garth's mouth, while Phat Rat loosened two of the tie-downs and unzipped the bag from the bottom until it was open to Garth's waist. As Garth screamed (as well as he could) into the shotgun barrels, Phat Rat undid Garth's belt and yanked off his pants and underwear. When Phat Rat left and came back with a pair of pruning sheers, FD had to turn away. It was too much. Garth tried to enunciate, but he sounded indistinguishable from a kid humming into a kazoo.

"You want to ask him one more time?" said Phat Rat, kneeling between Garth's legs. "Or should I snip some of it off first?"

Garth hummed some more and flopped like a fish.

FD turned around with difficulty. "You gonna give me the password?"

Garth nodded his head vigorously. Boom pulled the gun from his mouth. "Capital M-A-G-A, then lowercase f-o-r-e-v-e-r. *Please* don't cut my dick off!"

"MAGA forever?" Phat Rat said. "Are you fucking kidding me?"

Once the password worked, FD sighed in relief and got Garth some water, which he poured into Garth's mouth using a small plastic cup. Phat Rat again secured Garth's legs in the sleeping bag, while

Boom put the racquetball back in his mouth, reapplied the duct tape, and slipped the bag back over his head.

They then sat in silence while FD poked around the computer for anything that might help their mission. Although FD had spent two years fixing computers at Best Buy and had hacked into countless computers in his spare time, he expected Garth's laptop might present a special challenge. The White House network is "air gapped" with the outside internet, so there was no way he could remotely access any secure information, even with Garth's credentials—unless Garth was stupid enough to download it onto his computer.

It took FD three minutes to find Garth's former Backwater Mercenaries email account and another private email account that was apparently being used by ALT Task Force leadership to conduct White House business. Between the two accounts, there were nearly ten thousand emails. Surely something in there would help them.

"You'd think you'd know better, for all the shit you fucking people gave Hillary for using a private email server."

Garth mumbled something unintelligible beneath the hood. Boom conked him gently on the head with the shotgun barrel, just to remind him it was there.

FD put on his ear buds. The thumbing beat and raucous screams of Minor Threat blasted out everything from his mind but Garth's two email accounts. He scrolled the subjects, opening anything that seemed promising. Once he identified the senders and recipient, he honed his searches to just the ones that were likely to have helpful information. Many of the directives came from Stanley Congdon himself, as well as Officer John Meyer, who was now the lead law enforcement coordinator for the ALT Task Force's Washington Region. Joe's name was mentioned in several emails related to the manhunt in Virginia, but FD dared not search for the rest of their names, lest it leave a digital trail. Whenever he found a lead, he texted the pertinent information to Beach and Joe so they could follow up on it. After an hour, although he couldn't find anything like an investigations file or a target list, he had found tidbits of information about dozens of local suspects in individual emails.

Around midnight, there was a knock on the motel window. Phat Rat held her Beretta to the door and looked out the peephole.

FD took out one of his ear buds. "That's my man. Let him in."

Phat Rat unlatched the door, and Joe slipped inside, hood pulled low over his face, silent as a ninja. He smiled at Phat Rat, nodded at Boom, snatched Garth's bag from the bed, and left without saying a word.

Boom eventually fell asleep on the bed beside Garth, mumbling to himself throughout what seemed to be a nightmare involving the police.

Phat Rat sat perfectly still, gun in her lap, and smiled whenever FD looked up at her. He smiled back. In his mind, he resigned to make love to her when they were through. Inside Phat Rat's hard exterior was plainly a woman aching for love; inside FD was a man aching to share his love. It was the most natural thing in the world.

But then he chided himself: confusing pussy for love makes the world poorer. It breeds unwanted children. It pollutes the halls of apartment buildings with the cries of domestic anguish. No, he might *fuck* Phat Rat later—maybe—but that was all.

When he got all he could from the emails, he perused Garth's personal files. It was ninety percent porn, with a smattering of family photos, copies of utility bills, and other uninteresting junk. A file with a nonsensical name caught his eye. He opened it and nearly fell off the chair.

It was three pages from Donald Trump's autopsy report.

How would Garth have access to this? Of course, President Pence reopened the "investigation" into Trump's death with much fanfare. It was nothing but a thinly veiled attempt to feed meat to the conspiracy theorists while holding the threat of a trumped up (no pun intended) prosecution over the heads of would-be resisters. Naturally, the ALT Task Force was a part of the plot to pin Trump's death on the "alt-left." And Garth had been stupid enough to store part of the autopsy report on his personal laptop.

"What's perineal dermatitis?" FD said to himself.

Phat Rat laughed. "I think that's when you get a rash from having pee on you."

FD smirked at the word "cocaine," saved the autopsy report to his thumb drive, and sent an email from Garth's ALT Task Force account, careful to follow the syntax from Garth's real emails. He then shut the screen. He would drop the computer into the Potomac on their way back to D.C., but for now he and his two cohorts had done all they could do, short of cutting off Garth's dick. If FD's *other* nephews and nieces came through, if Beach could convince some of the suspects named in the emails to help them, if Joe could actually make it into Freedom City with Garth's credentials—and if he could poison the well, so to speak—then maybe, just maybe, they would drive the white shirts out of D.C. tomorrow morning.

For now, FD lay on the ground beside the bed, shut his eyes, and tried to get some rest before it all went down.

19. Freedom City

"What sort of name is Angus Daehniks?" The white shirt guarding the 7th Street entrance of Freedom City had the word "deplorable" tattooed on his neck, and his nametag identified him as "Travis S." He shined his flashlight at his clipboard and then at the tin badge on Joe's chest.

Joe lifted his cap to scratch his freshly cropped (but not, strictly speaking, shaved) head. Garth Simonson's white-shirt getup fit him perfectly. He had an olive drab duffel bag slung over his shoulder. "It's Gaelic. You implying I'm not white?"

The guard laughed. "Take it easy. You said Mr. Simonson sent you?"

"My name's on your list, ain't it?"

Travis pointed the flashlight at Joe's face. "You look familiar."

"I'm sure we used to run in the same circles."

"Where you from?"

"Texas. You?"

"Baton Rouge. You know Bill Carter from Killeen?"

Every white supremacist in Texas knew Bill Carter, who had been hosting rallies and concerts on his farm for thirty years. Joe nodded. "Yeah, I know him. I was at his wedding."

"His wedding? Shit, him and…"

"Amanda."

"Yeah, him and Amanda been married forever."

"It was about twelve years ago. I was the one who lit the cross after the ceremony."

"Shit, that was before my time. Must've been some wedding." Travis flicked off the light. "You must be tired. You gonna wanna head that way, three buildings down, and then hang a right toward the Warshington Monument. The guest bunks are in the Roger Taney building."

"Roger Taney, got it… Hey, I don't suppose I could get a bite to eat before I go to bed."

"Sure thing, Angus. The mess is just inside the camp on the Monument side, beside the chapel. The kitchen's closed now, but there are some vending machines in the cafeteria. The Sunday service is tomorrow morning at seven hundred, right after chow. Welcome to Freedom City!"

Joe passed between the gabion barriers, which were just short, plastic walls filled with sand. Although he had worked as an investigator in D.C. for a decade, the last time he had been on the National Mall—before the Capitol siege, that is—was when he took Naagesh to the Blossom Kite Festival. It had been daylight, springtime, festive, the entire sky dancing with colorful kites, children laughing, him and Geeta doing their best to keep Naagesh from being trampled. Now the Mall was dark, foreboding, cordoned off with walls, and its denizens were pure evil. Joe had no doubt that if Naagesh ever stumbled past these barriers, the white shirts would find a way to hurt him.

He passed the Roger Taney building—shaped like a giant, overturned can half-buried in the grass—and walked straight to the mess. The door was unlocked. Inside was a large cafeteria with folding tables and benches of the high school lunchroom variety. A row of vending machines encased one wall with nothing to offer but sodas, chips, and candy bars: real American food for *real* Americans. Along the opposite wall was a buffet line, with food basins—now empty—dish dispensers, refrigerated buffet display tables, and countertop warmers. Beyond the buffet line, now dark, was the kitchen. Joe donned rubber gloves and tried the handle of a door to the left of the buffet. It was locked. He tossed his duffel bag over one of the empty food basins and pulled himself over.

The freezer was locked too. But he found what he was looking for inside a cabinet behind the buffet line, beneath the industrial coffee maker: two fifty-pound bags of pre-ground coffee. He set his duffel bag on the tiles, fished through it until he found a plastic jug, and dumped half of the jug's contents in each of the coffee bags. The liquid was seven thousand dollars worth of PCP, supplied by one of FD's nephews and paid for with Beach's savings. Although Joe also had a smaller jar of LSD (street value: about five thousand dollars), he was unsure how it would react to the heat of the coffee maker. On the other hand, people smoke PCP all the time, so heat obviously doesn't affect its potency. Next, he found an unlocked pantry. There, he produced a syringe from his bag and injected some of the LSD into scores of apples, oranges, and bananas.

He then closed the pantry, hopped back over the buffet line, and crossed the lane to the "Reverend Jerry Falwell Jr. Chapel," which was as big as a high school gymnasium. He waited outside and listened for any sign of activity: nothing but the wind. Above the gabion barriers to the south, he saw the headlights of an occasional vehicle pass by on Independence Avenue. Otherwise, the Mall and its temporary denizens were sleeping. He tried the chapel entrance. It opened. He smiled to himself and slipped inside, closing the way behind him.

Behind the altar was a large stage, with guitars, a drum set, several massive amplifiers, expensive lighting (now off), and a podium with a microphone. He crept through the pews, past the stage, down one of the makeshift transepts, until he came to a door marked, "Reverend Harvey Smith - Office." He listened and then tried the handle. It turned. He nudged the door open with a squeak. Someone was snoring inside. He froze. A man coughed. A bed creaked. Joe counted silently in his head. Only when he counted to five hundred, when he heard regular breathing again, did he gently pull the door shut.

He returned to the stage and walked down the transept on the other side of the altar. Here he found an unmarked door, tried it, and this time he hit the jackpot. This room contained shelves of books, vestments, and other church supplies. He set the open boxes of sacramental wafers in rows on the carpet, and retrieved his jar of LSD from the duffel bag. He filled the syringe and squirted a couple drops on each wafer. The liquid discolored them a bit, but it was hardly noticeable. He used what was left in the jar on the closed packets of wafers, perforating the plastic packages with the needle. The dosages wouldn't be equal, but who cared?

LSD jar empty, he whispered into his radio: "Hallelujah. Service is at seven o'clock. Best plan for eight."

"Copy that," came the reply.

He shut off the radio, slipped out of the chapel, and returned to the Roger Taney building. Past a small foyer was a rectangular hall with rows of bunk beds. Named after the architect of the Dred Scott decision, the building was fittingly squalid, with a sticky floor, loud snoring, and the stench of a locker room. Joe felt his way down the dark aisles until he found an empty cot away from the loudest snorer. There, he set his bag beneath the bottom bunk and lay down, still wearing his clothes and boots. He closed his eyes and immediately fell into the deep sleep of someone whose conscience is single-mindedly clear.

He dreamed of Naagesh. In his dream, his son was still a year old. They were at the playground near the apartment in Arlington he had shared with Geeta. He was pushing Naagesh in a swing. Joe's father was standing there too.

His father held Naagesh's leg and stopped the swing. "You made yourself a little A-rab." To his father, racial identification went thusly: anyone who is not obviously black, white, or Asian falls into one of two categories: "spic" or "A-rab."

Joe started to jerk his son away from his father, but he was afraid if he yanked too hard it would hurt Naagesh's leg. He froze. His father always made him do that. When Joe was young it had been his sister who figuratively served the purpose of Naagesh's leg. His father implied something would happen to her if Joe ever stood up for himself. The threat worked.

In the dream, Naagesh began to cry. His father was sneering at him, clutching the boy's ankle. Joe let go of the chains and lunged around the swing to make his father let go. But when he let go of the chains, some terrible force yanked them and Naagesh shot away from him, overhead. The boy was still in the swing. Joe couldn't see what was pulling the chains. His father laughed. Joe punched him right in the teeth. There was a "crunch." He pulled back his hand. His father kept laughing. His teeth were bloody.

The chapel bells woke Joe with a start at seven o'clock.

"Shit." He rolled out of bed and rubbed his eyes.

"You missed chow," said a passing white shirt.

Joe stood, stretched his limbs, grabbed his duffel bag, and walked outside. The sun was just starting to rise above the Capitol, now under repair and covered with scaffolding. He held a hand above his eyes to shield them from the beautiful orange glare, and he grinned. Scores of white shirts shuffled between the rows of temporary buildings toward the chapel. Generators buzzed. Bleached polo shirts, pressed khakis, sweat-stained red hats, soulless eyes, soulless gaits, heartless cavities: Joe joined the troves marching to the chapel, just another warm body in America's army of deplorable bloodsuckers.

The Reverend Jerry Falwell Jr. Chapel was packed when he arrived. At least five hundred white shirts now filled the cushy pews, red hats in laps, a few shaved heads glowing under the blinding stage lights. Joe took a seat in the far back, tucking his duffel bag between his feet. Everyone there was between eighteen and thirty, making him likely the oldest person, except for the Reverend Harvey Smith. The preacher—in his late sixties, obese, with a conservative gray haircut—mulled about the stage as the band (dressed in the same white-shirt getup as everyone else) tuned their guitars.

The band turned out to be very shoddy imitation of AC/DC, with a message that was equal parts evangelical, nationalist, and apocalyptical. The words to their songs scrolled down several large monitors placed around the church. Joe followed along, trying to hide his incredulity. Besides the need to constantly praise and glorify God, other themes included the belief that Christ sent Pence to save Americans from sin, and that liberals are Satan's minions determined to destroy America. As they droned on, offbeat, out of tune, out of touch, some of the white shirts in the pews raised their hands in a bizarre amalgamation of a dab, a touchdown pose, and a "seig heil."

After three songs, the band stepped aside and Reverend Smith took the microphone. He pounded the podium with his fists as he preached about the "liberal scourge" and the need for everyone to accept Jesus Christ as their Lord and Savior.

"And you must never discuss religion with any group that considers any writing other than the Bible. That's how you pick up heretical ideas. That's how *Satan* gets his claws in you..."

Thirty minutes into the sermon, as Reverend Smith prattled on about sin and egoism—oozing with manipulation, superciliousness, and improbability—Joe was ready to ram a pen into his ear canal, just to make it stop. When it was time for communion, Joe stood in line and drank a sip of the wine, but he waived off the wafer due to "glutton allergies." When everyone had returned to his seat, the band played another song, and then Reverend Smith resumed preaching.

It was during the scriptural exegesis that a white shirt beside Joe abruptly dropped to his knees and yelled, "Trump lives!"

Joe watched the man, who stretched out his arms as if he were being crucified. Was this the first signs of the PCP kicking in? It seemed too soon for the LSD to have hit anyone yet, but as the whole sermon already had the hallmarks of an acid trip, it was hard to say.

"Praise Jesus!" someone near the front shouted.

Dozens more held their arms aloft, chanting, "Trump lives! Trump lives!"

Reverend Smith at first seemed to support the interruption, pausing for a moment to allow the chanting to die down on its own, but after a gulp of water he cleared his throat and continued the sermon, raising his voice to be heard above the fervent white shirts.

"The Devil!" someone screamed.

"Where?"

By Joe's estimation, the evocation of the Devil was his signal to skedaddle. He looked at his watch—7:47 a.m., a tad early—but it was close enough. He stood and nudged his way to the exit. From his bag he removed two tear gas canisters: Fox Labs 5.3M SHU police pepper spray grenades (less than thirty bucks apiece at the local gun store).

He engaged the "continuous discharge" lock on one of the grenades and hurled it into the center of the chapel. Noxious chemicals filled the pews. White shirts howled in agony. The canister spun in circles. One man tried to pick it up, but instead ended up kicking it across the aisle in true slapstick fashion.

Joe engaged the lock on the second grenade and dropped it right inside the entrance. As an afterthought he screamed, "Fearless Vampire Killers!"

Then he slammed the door and ran.

His eyes burned from the pepper spray in the air. He struggled to keep them open. Snot ran down his face. He paused for a moment to yank off his shirt, which he held over his nose and mouth. He pulled out his last pepper spray can and left his bag on the ground. He sprinted for the closest exit on Independence Avenue.

"Stop him!" someone yelled.

He charged for the checkpoint. A white shirt reared a club over his head, prepared to smack Joe like a baseball. Joe sprayed him in the eyes. The man howled, covered his face, and dropped to the ground, where he writhed like a fat worm. Joe darted around him, hopped over the gabion barrier, and landed on the sidewalk outside of Freedom City.

The crowd seemingly appeared out of nowhere, crossing Independence Avenue en masse. There were hundreds of them: men, women, transgendered; young and old; and black, white, and every hue in between. Some had masks and carried weapons—he saw a few baseball bats and a tire iron—but most were unarmed, even bare-armed, sleeves rolled up, ordinary citizens who had had enough of Freedom City and who had come to take their city back. How on earth had the others managed to raise such a massive army overnight? As the crowd approached the sidewalk, Joe cheered and waved his shirt in the air.

Then a woman punched him in the head.

"I'm on your side!" he said.

Someone kicked him in the leg. "If you're gonna be a Nazi—then at least have the courage of conviction to admit when you're a Nazi!"

"I'm *not* a Nazi!"

"Then why you waving a white shirt?"

Joe was surrounded, jostled, and shoved. A fist connected with his chin. He tripped to the ground and curled into a ball.

Then a naked man ran by.

Joe opened an eye and recognized the streaker from his ID card. It was Garth Simonson—now completely free, both figuratively and in fact. The crowd assailing Joe turned and gawked as Garth—square-jawed, powerfully built, tiny penis wiggling—sprinted past, straight through the checkpoint of Freedom City. Citizens were now streaming through the checkpoints, as the white shirts were in no condition to stop them.

Crowd momentarily distracted, Joe sprang up and darted away, down Independence Avenue. Hundreds of others were gathered near the Washington Monument, ready to descend on the camp. Sirens wailed in the distance. He tossed the polo shirt in a gutter and made his way, shirtless, toward Memorial Bridge. Behind him, the sun shined for the last time over Freedom City as the citizens of D.C. began the task of tearing it down piece-by-piece. The police and the army might try to stop them, but there were thousands of resisters now and they were determined to take back their city—to take back America—to run the fascists back into their holes.

He was sad he couldn't stay around to see if a revolution would take hold, to watch President Pence deposed, to watch Stanley Congdon and the likes of him ostracized, tried, convicted, imprisoned, and ultimately forgotten, except as an embarrassing blip in a history book. Now a wanted man, Joe was heading to rejoin his family in India by way of Mexico, if he wasn't first caught or killed. He may never return.

He hadn't made it too far past the Washington Monument, when a black Impala pulled up beside him. The driver's window lowered.

"Need a ride, Jack?" FD said. "Beach and Clare are waiting for us."

Joe took one last look behind him, at the chaos and the glaring sun, truth, hope: America. He got in the car, and they zoomed across the Memorial Bridge, where a cop was already starting to block traffic into the city. Joe gave him the finger as they passed.

20. The Getaway

As the exits passed one after another, back to the I-81, then the I-40—seemingly forever, all the way to Little Rock—the permanence of their impending farewell set like a stone in Clare's stomach, twisting it into a tight knot. They were now driving a white Dodge panel van ("borrowed") with two bikes tied in the cargo area, and they had not stopped for sixteen hours except to refuel. It was dark outside, and it was FD's turn at the wheel. Clare sat in the passenger seat, listening to the radio, staring out at the abundant red taillights, brooding.

According to the news, Freedom City had indeed been torn apart in the melee. Regrettably, one white shirt was beaten to death, others hospitalized. The police and military rounded up hundreds of "alt-left" rioters, but thousands of others, including the masterminds, had escaped. Only one suspect was named publicly: Joseph Kaline.

Of course, President Pence pledged to rebuild Freedom City, but cynical commentators pointed out that the optics weren't good. They described images (not visible on the radio) of confused white shirts, apparently under the influence of some psychotropic or psychedelic drug, running the streets of D.C., screaming about "the Devil" and "vampires," and trying to hide from the mobs. The czar's own deputy, one Garth Simonson, was recorded streaking naked across the National Mall.

Even the conservative pundits were asking, "What sort of circus was Stanley Congdon running over there?"

As far as the Fearless Vampire Killers were concerned, it was critically important that they first get Joe as close as possible to the Mexican border, because every cop in America was looking for him now. Beach had given him ten thousand dollars to help him find his way across the Atlantic and hopefully reunite with his wife and son in India. They were planning on stopping near San Antonio to see his sister. Although Joe knew it was a risk, he wanted to say goodbye to her before he left the country forever.

Although cagey about his specific plans, FD would take the van and start a new life for himself somewhere in the West. With his grandmother gone, he had no actual family left in D.C., just his myriad "nephews" and girlfriends. Clare suspected he was heading to Los Angeles, but she knew better than to ask him. Wherever he was going was his own business, and it was better that she didn't know.

As for her and Beach, they would ride their bikes back to Austin, in order to experience what Joe told them was one of the South's few cool cities. Unlike the rest of them, she had not entirely written off the South. She wanted to see some live music, dance, relax, eat phenomenal Tex-Mex, and meet people who reaffirmed her faith in America and in humanity.

But would she ever again find people like FD and Joe?

"I'm gonna see if I can get some sleep." She edged her way into the cargo area, where she found Beach and Joe laying side by side between the bikes, surrounded by their abundant bags of food and camping gear. "Anyone want to sit up front for a while?"

Beach pulled himself up. Nearly two weeks without a drink, and he was looking sturdier already. "I'll keep FD company, maybe take a turn at the wheel."

Clare stretched out beside Joe, propped a bag beneath her head, and pulled a blanket up to her chin. The van rattled and creaked. Outside cars flew past them at intervals.

"I'm going to miss you most of all," he said.

She scooted closer to him and put her head on his chest. "I'm going to miss you too."

He played with her hair. Even with all the noise outside she could hear his heart beating. This was it: their last few hours together. As much as they had accomplished, as much as they shared, she was never going to see Joe again. She slipped her hand beneath his shirt and rested it on his chest, over his heart.

"Why do you do this? Sleep around like you do?"

She pulled his chest hair. "You're fucking *married*, Joe. You're going back to your wife. Don't judge me."

He put his hands on her shoulders, massaging her muscles, soothing her. "You're right. I'm sorry."

They removed their shirts and rubbed their tummies together. She looked in his eyes. They were concerned, loving eyes. Their noses were nearly touching. He had a bruise on his cheek from where the mob assaulted him. She glanced down at his arm and noticed his scar for the first time, where his skin was raw and badly pocked, as if it

118

had been scorched. She traced her finger along the crescent that formed the lower outline: the shape of a frying pan.

"What happened to you here?" she asked.

"I used to be one of them."

"And now you're not."

"And now I'm not." He kissed her mouth. She closed her eyes and chewed on his lower lip, until he asked, "Do you love Beach?"

She met his eyes. "Yes."

"Do you love FD?"

"In a way. I love you in a way too."

"Okay, I'm sorry. It's just that if you were mine, truly mine... well, you'd just be mine."

"I know."

They wiggled out of their jeans and rubbed their tummies together more, kissing, until the friction made her wet and made him hard, drove them both mad. He disappeared beneath the blanket. His mouth found her neck, closed on her nipples, left a trail of saliva down her tummy, lingered on her hipbones—lower, lower. His lips kissed her thighs, her kneecaps, her feet—higher, higher—until his teeth grazed her clit and his tongue was pressing her against the floor. The van rumbled. She pressed her thighs around his shorn head and came hard.

"Texarkana ahead!" Beach declared from the front.

She rode Joe across the Texas border, until they collapsed back beneath the blanket, arms and legs entangled, panting and sweaty.

"You know you could come see me in India someday, assuming I make it there."

"If you weren't married it might be different." She nuzzled her head beneath his chin and drank in his pheromones for perhaps the last time. "Hey, if you used to be one of them and you changed, maybe there's still hope for America."

"Maybe," He kissed her forehead. "As long as there's still someone here to fight for it."

21. Sunset in the Desert

Boiling in the heat, in the abundant brownness, the sweltering, squalid sameness of some trailer park outside San Antonio, every cell in Beach's body positively craved a cool, refreshing martini. Salty hint of olive, invigorating juniper berries, gin: if he had to live another day without a drink, he was prepared to die now and get it over with. Their drive through the South had convinced him the war for America was already lost. The liberal intellectuals of the West and Northeast were sorely outnumbered by the droves of dumb rednecks. Ceding Texas back to Mexico and carving Florida off into the Caribbean Sea would be a start, but then what to do with inland Kentucky and Oklahoma? Nuke them? He didn't want *that* kind of blood on his hands.

He had paid off Sarah to represent Clare, should she ever need it. He would make sure she got back to D.C. or Vermont—or wherever. She had this wild notion of riding their bikes through the desert. He would do it because he loved her, although he knew now he could never keep up with her.

They would first make sure Joe got to the border. Beach had given him some money so he might find his way to India. Beach had given FD an equal amount to start over again somewhere in the West.

Then what?

Maybe Beach would drink himself into a stupor until his liver gave out. He had had a good run. His only regret was that he would never witness President Pence's impeachment or live to see the Nationals win the World Series.

Joe sprinted around the corner of his sister's trailer, eyebrows creased with foreboding, face slick with sweat. He hopped in the van and slammed the door. "That didn't go well. They're going to call the cops on me—no doubt about it. We need to get moving."

From around the corner emerged a dark-haired man in a wife-beater shirt, jailhouse tattoos on his arms. A short woman, hair done up like a well-coifed orangutan, stamped along behind the dark-haired man, trying to tug his arm back in the opposite direction. Beach pulled a U-turn, waved as they passed the couple, and skidded out of the trailer park.

"What happened?" Clare asked from the back of the van.

"That guy she's seeing is a serious asshole—and he's a Trump supporter."

There was nothing left to say. Joe had wanted to say goodbye to his sister, even though they all knew it was a risk. Now the police were going to know what kind of vehicle they were driving, if not also the tag number.

Joe slammed a hand down on the dashboard. "I should've had you park farther away. I'm sorry."

FD's big head popped out of the back. "Don't beat yourself up about it, Joe. That's your family. We can pick up new tags once we put some distance between us and San Antonio."

Beach turned onto Route 90 eastbound, and they drove seemingly forever with only the redundant drone of the radio news. They stole tags from a similar van at a truck stop outside Uvalde, putting their old ones on the other vehicle. That would prevent anyone from noticing for a while. They then swept past Del Río (too obvious a border crossing site), over the majestic Amistad Reservoir, and turned northward into the wild, rolling desert. Pausing momentarily to consult their map, Beach turned down a dusty path, drove at a slow crawl for fifteen miles until they met a dead end, where the "road," as it were, ran smack into a grove of cactuses as big as oak trees. He turned off the motor. On the right was a sand dune the size of a small shopping mall. Ahead, beyond the cactuses, the sun was setting somewhere over the Mexican border: a line of orange like molten lava melting into an outrageous pink candy explosion.

FD whistled. "Now, that's something to see."

They climbed from the van, stretched their legs, and watched the sliver of vibrant colors grow thinner and dimmer, until the colors disappeared and only a swatch of lighter blue remained on the horizon.

Beach put one arm around FD and the other around Joe. "Being that this is literally the end of the road, it's probably as good a place as any to part ways." He pulled his arm from Joe's shoulder and gestured to the still-light sky. "You're following the sun." He took his arm from FD and smacked it lightly on the van's hood. "You just need to backtrack a ways until you're on Route 90 again… Clare and I, we got about, what? Three hundred miles—ride back to Austin…"

She folded her arms around him. "It will be good for you. Clean out the toxins in your body."

FD peeled his eyes, wet with tears, from the seemingly endless desert and embraced Joe. "You gonna make it past the border, man?"

"It's just a lot of desert and a big-ass river. I brought an innertube. You're the one who needs to be careful, because the cops are looking for the van by now. Definitely stay off the main highways."

"I'll ditch it as soon as I can." FD hugged Beach and then Clare. "You guys be careful out there on them roads."

Joe dabbed his eyes, yanked open the van's rear doors, and began dragging out his gear. "Ef-dee's right. People out here don't respect bicycles like they do in D.C. You gotta stay well off the road, or they'll clip you and leave you for dead."

Clare lifted her bike from the back, leaned it against the van, and blew her nose on a dirty shirt. The saddlebags were already packed full with their camping stuff, abundant food, and enough water to last them three days, before they could find a place to refill their canteens. Beach pulled out his bike too, keeping his upper lip stiff.

FD clapped him on the back. "You sure you guys don't at least wanna ride back to the main road?"

"No, thanks. We've got plenty of water. Might as well spend our first night somewhere pretty."

Joe strapped on his pack, a coil of rope dangling off the side. "Adios, amigos. I got a long way to go."

One last group hug, eight toes pointed at each other in the dust, teardrops accumulating between them: "The end of an era," Beach said.

He then put his arm around Clare and together they watched Joe's silhouette fade off between the cactuses. The engine roared back to life, FD honked, waved, and soon the old ghost of a panel van disappeared into a cloud of fine dust. Clare threw her hands over her face and sobbed. Beach put his arms around her and let himself go too. They held each other, letting their tears water the cactuses, until staying still any longer seemed like undue torture. He kissed her tears. She kissed his too. With the sun gone there was a chill in the air.

He fished out his Harry Potter cloak from one of his saddlebags, tied it around his neck. "We might as well ride a few miles before we set up camp."

She laughed. "You're ridiculous."

They switched on their lights and set off in the direction FD had just gone. The fine dust he had kicked up with the van's tires still hung in the air, stinging Beach's eyes and causing a slight burn in the back of his throat. Even with the headlight, it was difficult to avoid the abundant holes in the road. He could no better keep up with Clare in the desert than he could in the urban jungle of D.C. He pedaled as long as he could, but she was quickly far ahead of him, a tiny blip of a red light far off up the road. Even the dust had dissipated, until it was just him and the cold air. A tumbleweed rolled past him—a fucking tumbleweed! What on earth led him here? Was he even still *on* earth?

His bicycle's seat loosened, forcing him to pedal in short little circles like he was riding a kid's bike. Then his cloak caught in the rear tire. He untangled it, tucked the back of it into his belt, and rode on, alone, for another hour, until he found her waiting for him beside a massive cactus shaped like a pitchfork.

She laughed. "You look like an elephant on a unicycle."

He fell off the bike and lay on his back in the dirt beside her, looking up at the stars. There were thousands of them, clear as diamonds on black velvet. "If I make it back to D.C. alive, I'm going to give up drinking."

"You already gave up drinking."

"I mean for good."

She examined his loose bicycle seat. "We need one of those Ikea wrenches."

"Only a white woman from Massachusetts would call an Allen wrench an 'Ikea wrench.'"

"I'm from Vermont, asshole."

"Vermont, Massachusetts—it's all going to the enemy anyway."

She leaned the bike against the cactus and sat beside him in the sand. "We just got started, but it's going to get easier the farther we go. You'll see."

"Do you think we've done any good? We've been fighting them, but there'll always be about a third of the American population that's basically mentally retarded."

She slapped his head. "People don't say 'mentally retarded' anymore. It's offensive."

"I meant it in a clinical sense."

"Regardless, it's an offensive and inaccurate comparison."

"My only problem with the P.C. revolution is there aren't any fitting pejoratives anymore. I tell you, the only good thing millennials ever did was bring back beards."

She lay down, draped her arms around him, and stuck her nose in his beard. "You're just upset because your time has already passed."

He turned to her and smiled. "Anyone ever tell you you're perspicacious for a millennial?"

She laughed—and then she shot to her feet and pointed to a faint light on the horizon. "Helicopter!"

"What?"

He followed her eyes and could see a spotlight pointed at the earth, moving toward them. A dust cloud raged beneath the light. They vaulted onto their bikes, switched off their lights, and pedaled back in the direction they had come. Maybe they could find a place to hide among the cactuses? Clare outpaced him, again. Without a light, with his seat broken, he crashed repeatedly in the holes and sand, hopping back on, doing his best to keep up with her, to survive. But within a minute she was fifty feet away, then a hundred feet. He could no longer see her at all. Meanwhile, the telltale "whook-whook" of chopper blades beat the air behind him. He could sense the spotlight drawing nearer.

And then it was on him.

The blades beat up a massive cloud of dust that swirled around him like hellfire.

He squinted into the light and couldn't make out a damn thing. What did it matter? He was caught. But maybe if they stopped to detain him Clare could still escape? She was in phenomenal shape. She could ride her bike for four days straight. She might catch up with Joe and make it to Mexico.

He waved his arms, trying to get the chopper to land, to bide her more time. But it didn't move. It just hovered, unfeeling and soulless—just another tool in the fascist's arsenal. The spotlight turned for a moment and he could see the "U.S. Border Patrol" logo on one side and the silhouette of a machine-gun turret. He put up his hands in a sign of unconditional surrender.

"Come and get me, you motherfucking fascists!"

The light enveloped him again, and he felt a sharp pain in his stomach, followed by the unmistakable discharge of a firearm. It felt like Jayson Werth hit him in the gut with a baseball bat.

He dropped to his knees and put his hands to his shirt. His fingers came back red. Blood poured onto the sand. He fell backward, faced toward his destiny. It was as good a place to die as any, better than languishing in a hospice for a year. Someone shook his shoulders.

"You fucking bastards!" Clare screamed.

"Run!" he tried to say, but he was already losing consciousness and the word got caught in his throat.

The light grew dimmer, the atmosphere quieter, until Clare's sobs sounded like they came from far beneath the sand and the "whook-whook" grew slower and slower, until it stopped completely.

22. Loving

Alone again, a solitary monk—known as "Ace" by those who once called themselves the Fearless Vampire Killers—FD coasted to the side of Route 285, a mile past the New Mexico border. The engine died, and it was just as well. He had been lucky thus far—but nothing in the world is as fickle as luck. He let the inertia propel him, until a single grain of sand gave the last iota of friction required to bring the van to a dead stop.

Over the past two days he had stayed off the I-10, the only interstate for hundreds of miles. Last night he had camped at the bottom of a ridge near Iraan, Texas, falling asleep to the sound of churning oil pumps at the nearby Yates Oil Field. Having lived his entire life in D.C., he expected Western Texas to be nothing but sweat, bad radio stations, endless sand, oil fields, scrub grass, many farms, and a thousand small towns with stupid names—invariably centered around a ginormous church. It was these things, but it was also much more.

While he had planned on tearing through Texas, New Mexico, and Arizona as fast as he could and settling in a Californian metropolis, probably Los Angeles or San Diego, he continued to see things in the Southwest that made him pause and reexamine his prejudices. The impossibly beautiful sunsets; a small brick memorial for someone killed in a car accident in the middle of nowhere, the inscription "He was my world" etched above a freshly plucked yucca flower; and a lonesome cowboy riding a horse along the road, smoking a cigar, grocery bags tied to his saddle: there was abundant art here, for those whose eyes were open to it.

Why, even in Iraan—a town whose name he had written off as idiotic—someone at a gas station told him it was so called when its founder Ira joined his name with his wife Ann's. After that, FD spent the morning laughing out loud at what his own town might be called if he ever found a soul mate. Some of the names didn't sound too bad—"Effare," for example, and "Langette"—but the women in the suffixes weren't right for him. Perhaps the woman's name could be the prefix?

He was chuckling over the harmonics of "Phatdee" when the van broke down.

He got out, opened the hood, and scratched his head at the engine for good measure. He checked the oil: still black. He tugged the leads to the battery: still secure. He kicked the tires: still buoyant. On his left was a mountain range ending in a sharp peak at the summit. Part of the summit had obviously broken off, making it look like elephants had trampled on it. He stared down the road and mentally prepared himself for standing with his thumb out, forever, until he was either arrested or killed—quite literally—from racism.

Then he bleached the car clean inside and out, so as not to leave a trace of DNA or fingerprints, emptied everything he could fit into his backpack, and hiked along the highway, sweating profusely, brutal sun bearing down on him. Although his skin was too dark to burn, it felt like someone had lit a campfire in his copious hair.

It took him two hours to reach some semblance of civilization, a gas station in Loving, New Mexico. There, drenched in sweat, salt stains lining his black t-shirt, he filled his canteens in the bathroom and browsed the shelves as an excuse to stay in the air conditioning for just a few more minutes. The proprietor—male, obese, shorn in overalls—watched him from the corner of his eye, the other eye on a TV that was blaring Fox "News." The anchor, a blond woman with huge, silicone breasts, was whirring on about the "leftwing terrorists" who had organized the attack on Freedom City. FD listened, but tried not to seem too interested.

A pudgy Native American woman, skin like amber and smooth black hair—adorned with three eagle feathers—entered and smiled at him. His heart quickened, but he was sure it was just because he was relieved to see another brown person. She wore rainbow flip-flops and a tube top. She caught him looking at her belly and quickly turned away to pre-pay for gas.

He continued browsing the shelves. They contained mostly the regular stuff: candy bars, energy bars, "health" bars, and other highly processed, plastic-encased foods. He recalled Clare once saying, "Americans like their food already chewed up for them." Without skipping a beat, Beach had replied, "Pretty soon food will be consumed via plastic-encased suppositories, inserted straight into our butts." FD chortled at the memory, drawing a glare from the proprietor.

Beside the sweet food was a small rack of non-consumable sundries, including various New Mexico themed trucker caps and a few items "Made by *Real* Native Americans!" He picked up a necklace that was just a leather string through an arrowhead. The arrowhead felt like it was actually made of rock. He looked at the tag. It claimed it had been made at the Mescalero Apache Reservation.

He held up the necklace to the proprietor. "Hey, how far we from the Apache Reservation?"

"About three hours, if you're driving." The man looked FD up and down, focusing on his hair and then on the backpack. "It's about a hundred-fifty miles if you're walking."

FD thanked him and kept stalling. The Native American woman left to go fill up her tank.

"Authorities have not yet released the names of the two people in custody, but our sources describe them as a man and a woman who were trying to cross the Mexican border. Police are still on the hunt for their ringleader, Joseph Kaline, and an unidentified African American man, seen here in this police sketch…"

The arrowhead necklace clattered to the floor. FD glanced at the screen and saw a digital sketch of an African American man wearing a ski mask. Thankfully, only his eyes were visible—but they were surprisingly well done. He knew those eyes well, for they were just like his father's. Funny, he thought, how seeing something in a different way, in isolation, could change one's perspective. He had not realized how much their eyes were the same.

When the channel went on a commercial break, he asked as cheerily as he could muster, "How much for a hat?"

With his new "Loving, New Mexico" hat—unclasped on the back to make room for his ample hair—he left the gas station. The wall of humidity felt like an unwanted hug on the Fourth of July. He passed the Native American woman, who was filling the tank of a beat-up, brown Jeep Wrangler. He then skulked off toward the mountains.

Beach and Clare's capture saddled FD with a profound sadness. Coupled with the oppressive heat, it made his feet heavy and sapped his will to continue. Sweat poured from his body. How was he going to hike another hundred and fifty miles in the desert? How was he going to survive without his fellow Fearless Vampire Killers?

He was weighing whether to return to the gas station to turn himself in, when the Jeep pulled beside him and the woman called out, "I overheard you're going to Mescalero. You heading to the casino?"

"I don't gamble."

"Well, you don't look like a golfer either, so that must mean you're not going *to* there as much as you're going *from* somewhere else." She looked at his eyes. "You look familiar. You famous?"

"I hope not."

"Want a ride to Mescalero?" He nodded and wiped the sweat from his forehead. She reached over to open the door for him. He hefted his bag in the backseat and climbed in the front. "I'm Azul," she said. "I'm in the Chiricahua band of the Mescalero tribe, a direct descendant of Geronimo."

"My name's Ef-dee."

"Don't know what you're searching for, Ef-dee—but maybe I can take you a step ahead of whatever it is you're running from."

She pushed the gas and started again up Route 285. The Jeep's top was off, but there was a covering that protected them from the sun, and the breeze felt wonderful. He was so glad he hadn't turned himself in. For a while he watched the dunes roll past, the cactuses, the distant mountains—but eventually his eyes rested on Azul.

"Do you mind if I draw you?" he asked.

She laughed. "Knock yourself out."

He reached into the back and pulled out a sketchpad and a pen from his backpack. As he put pen to paper, her eagle feathers rippled in the wind. Her hair, now tied in a ponytail, danced along her upper back. Her neck and her arms glistened from the sticky air. FD sketched these things in motion, beauty unfolding in real time. She glanced at him occasionally and smiled. With a deft line he recorded her lovely smirk. With a smear of his fingertip he recorded her eye's first twinkle of curiosity.

Her eyes told him a lot: he was certain now he could fuck her if he chose to. The perspiration on her chest made his tongue hang out. But also he felt a pull in his chest, something that was not purely carnal. There was a story behind Azul's flirtatious eyes that FD suddenly had to learn. It was antithetical to his nature to ask questions—women usually threw themselves at him first—but now he struggled to find the right words.

He took a deep breath and dove into love's first leap.

23. ¡Viva México!

On a cliff overlooking the Mexican border, Joe put on his harness, tied his rope to a tree, and belayed himself down to the Rio Grande River basin. Once at the bottom, he stepped out of his harness and left it dangling from the cliff, making it easy for the next lucky migrant to climb up. He then blew up his innertube, stepped into it, and waded into the river, doing his best to keep his pack above the water and his boots pointed downstream, to keep the rocks below from tearing his ass to shreds.

By the time he paddled across, he was a good half-mile further east than where he had started, but at least he was in Mexico. He filled his purifier with water, strained it through the filter, and poured it into his canteen. He then hiked south into the Mexican desert—which unsurprisingly looked just like the American desert. The sun was relentless, and he was sweating more liquid than he could drink.

He stopped at midday to rest in the meager shade of a solitary cactus. As he ate his lunch he had to scoot a few inches every five minutes to prevent the sun from hitting him. He kept an ear open for helicopters, internal combustion engines, and human voices. What he had not expected, however, was a man riding a horse. By the time Joe heard it, the horse and its rider were standing right over him. The sun cast them into complete shadows.

The man, wearing a sombrero, said in heavily accented but otherwise perfectly spoken English, "You a wetback?"

Joe shrugged. "I guess I am a wetback. You the Federales?"

"Something like that, but you can call me Pedro." He tipped his hat, momentarily blocking the sun so that Joe could make out the man's outrageously full, black mustache and a smile full of pearly teeth. "Where you headed?" Pedro asked.

"It's not so much where I'm heading, as where I'm leaving. Recent circumstances have made it impossible for me to stay in the U.S.A."

"So you're a refugee?"

"Um, sort of."

"Well, then you'll be happy to know that *our* immigration policies are much more lenient than what you have in the United

States. We don't make people fill out a lot of forms, or nothing like that. Once we know the refugee's name we simply ask him one question."

Joe nodded, expecting that he was about to part with some or all of Beach's cash he had stashed in his boots. "My name is… Harry."

"And whom did you vote for?"

"Hillary Clinton."

"Then, welcome to Mexico, Joseph Kaline." Pedro held out his hand and smiled. "I mean, Señor Harry. Come, I'll give you a ride to Ciudad Acuña."

"You know who I am? How did you find me?"

"Your police agencies aren't nearly as smart as they think they are. We didn't much like your scum-sucker Trump and his stupid wall idea."

Joe hoisted himself onto the back of Pedro's horse, and they rode three hours until they approached the dusty outskirts of Ciudad Acuña, where Pedro dropped him off outside a motel called El Motel Soñoliento del Gallo.

"The owner is named Jesus. Tell him I sent you, pay him what he asks, and he'll give you a room."

"I can't thank you enough!"

"It is nothing, but be careful in Ciudad Acuña, Señor Harry. There actually *are* some bad hombres here."

"There are bad hombres everywhere."

Pedro flashed a smile. "And good hombres too."

Joe watched the strange horseman canter down the empty street, then entered the office, where he found Jesus sleeping behind the counter. He told him Pedro sent him, paid fifty U.S. dollars, and received a room key with no questions asked.

Room 11 was on the upper level, up some stairs and down an exterior corridor that overlooked a courtyard strung with laundry lines. The room was basically a closet with one window and a bend to the right when you enter the room. He wiggled the Uzi from his backpack, careful not to shoot himself in the process, and set it on the ground beside the bed. He then wedged the only nightstand between the door and the corner of the wall. He plopped down on the bed, which was beneath the window. The air was sweltering. The mattress felt like a rock. He closed his eyes.

He dreamed again of Naagesh. This time they were swimming together in a grotto. Joe dove beneath the clear water and emerged to find his son perched on a slab of rock, watching him, staring at his tattoos.

"Papa, how come you hate me?"

Joe followed his son's eyes and realized with horror that his tattoos were still there, a swastika on his arm, the words "Blood and Soil" beneath it. He tried to twist around to see if the one on his back was still there, but he needed a mirror. He let himself slide beneath the water, until only his head was exposed, so his son wouldn't see his shame.

"I've never hated you. That was before I knew you, before I knew how much I could love someone. I never knew what love was before I met your mother."

His son began to cry and ran away. Joe hesitated because he didn't want to get out of the water where people would see him for what he was. But without getting out, he couldn't hold his son and tell him he loved him. He grabbed onto the edge of the rock and pulled himself up, dripping, onto the slab. He followed his son's wet footprints, which led around a pile of rocks.

Then there was a loud bang.

Joe's eyes popped opened. Another crash: the room's door buckled, but held against the nightstand.

It was still light outside. He heard pristine English—commands, cop talk. An armed silhouette scurried across the window. This was clearly not housekeeping. He snatched his gun from the floor and kept it trained on the window, expecting something or someone to crash through it.

Instead, they just started shooting.

The door exploded. Wood splintered. Sparks flew. Little holes appeared all over the wall opposite the door. Joe dove under the bed's wrought iron frame. The staccato of automatic weapons fire suggested a small army was outside.

When the shooting finally stopped he peered over the bed. Daylight shined through the smoke and dust. His first thought was that it was amazing the window was still intact and that exterior wall was still standing. The door, however, looked like a piece of Swiss cheese. He checked himself for injuries. Except his heart racing at an unhealthy and altogether unsustainable speed, he was unscathed.

"Viva la Mexico!" he shouted. He then stood and emptied his magazine through the window and into the wall, hoping to hit the enemy, whoever they were.

But this was a big mistake, for he realized—too late—the reason they missed him before was because the shooters didn't know about the bend in the room. They had been firing at the door, so their bullets had passed harmlessly through the wall (well, maybe not harmless to whoever happened to be in the next room). By shooting through the window, Joe had now told them exactly where to aim. The shouts outside, the guttural, confident voices of tough-talking American cops, confirmed his fear.

"Fuck!" He dove back under the bed.

The machine guns ripped the wall to pieces. The holes seemed to open up all at once. It instantly got much lighter in the room as the sunlight trailed behind the bullets. He could even see the legs of a man standing just on the other side of the wall, clad in urban camouflage, pumping bullets into this room. With an empty gun, Joe lay flat beneath his bed, waiting for the bullet that would ultimately pierce one of his vital organs.

24. American Hero

Officer John G. Meyer had been waiting for this day ever since he recognized that smug private detective in the hallway at D.C. Superior Court. That slimy dirtball had broken into his house, stolen eight hundred dollars of hard-earned bribes from his freezer, hacked into his computer, emptied his checking account, and even swiped his favorite porno DVD. By dredging up that whole Junior Smalls thing, that motherfucker had almost—almost—ended Officer Meyer's career. With pressure from that fat-assed prosecutor Cynthia Truitt, the MPD suspended him, with pay of course, pending an investigation. Thankfully, that didn't preclude him from detailing to the Alt-Left Terrorism Task Force, where he had found a second calling.

When the FBI found a DNA match on a drop of blood left on the base of the Robert E. Lee statue in Charlottesville, Officer Meyer knew that God had put him on the Task Force for one reason—and that reason was to send Joseph Fucking Kaline straight back to hell.

Now, here he was in Mexico—fucking Mexico—leading an elite team of American law enforcement officers (hand picked, all "Cops for Comeup-Pence"), and they were standing atop an exterior corridor and emptying their government issued, full-auto Heckler & Koch UMPs straight into the wall of the fugitive's motel room. The frantic drumbeat of gunshots was deafening. The .45 rounds ripped fist-size holes in the wall. Plaster exploded. Empty shells fell like raindrops onto the courtyard below. Revenge had never felt so exhilarating.

When he emptied his second magazine, he let it fall to the ground, jammed in another, and yanked the bolt release, slamming another round into the chamber. He kept it at the low ready and waited for his teammates to stop shooting. There was another burst of machine-gun fire, the clatter of spent shells, and then silence. It was almost time to go through the window.

When Joseph Fucking Kaline's sister had reported him in San Antonio, they called in extra eyes along the Mexican border. Officer Meyer and his team caught the first U.S. Army transport to Texas. When they spotted that attorney and his assistant riding their bikes in the desert it was just too easy. One shot in the gut for Mr. Beach

Sands, Esq.: an "accidental discharge." It happens. He had wanted to waste the bitch too, but that would have been too obvious. When they followed Joseph Fucking Kaline's tracks to the Rio Grande, Officer Meyer had called his supervisor and pleaded for permission to make the crossing.

His supervisor had had to check with Stanley Congdon, but even the czar couldn't order them to enter a sovereign country. Mr. Congdon had to check with the White House, with President Pence himself. After some delay, the President had given the go-ahead, but with one stipulation: Joseph Fucking Kaline was to be killed in Ciudad Acuña, not carted back across the border, alive, to be tried by a liberal jury in Northern Virginia—and certainly not left in Mexican custody. Fake news and liberal propaganda had caused the relationship between the two countries to deteriorate to one of barely contained acrimony.

As he waited for any signs of life inside (it was inconceivable they had not riddled their fugitive with a hundred bullets by now), he heard shouting down in the courtyard, Spanish shouting—Mexicans—in Mexico. What was the world coming to?

Officer Meyer knew exactly zero Spanish, but even he could understand, "Policía Federal!"

He stepped through the window frame, leapt into the motel room, and fell smack onto the bed. He jumped to his feet—standing atop the bed—and pivoted his gun around the tiny room. The air was more asbestos than air. The walls looked like Swiss cheese. He looked down. Two legs were poking out from beneath the frame. He aimed a sustained burst of machine-gun fire straight into the mattress, straight into Joseph Fucking Kaline's traitorous torso.

Hands then reached through the window and pulled him out into the corridor, onto the floor, onto his face.

"¡En el piso!" someone shouted.

"Stand down!" Officer Meyer called to his men, but as he looked up he saw they were already on the ground, disarmed, looking scared and dejected. The Federales—there were scores of them, clad in S.W.A.T. gear—frisked him, plucking guns and ammunition from his various pockets. "Easy fellas. We're police officers too, from the United States." He began to reach for his badge and his ALT Task Force credentials, but he felt a gun barrel against the back of his neck.

Then a bag was pulled over his head, and he was handcuffed and hogtied. He had no idea what anyone was saying. They carried him like a suitcase down the stairs and tossed him into what felt like the bed of a box truck. He heard his comrades thrown in too, with a grunt, one by one. A roll-up door was slammed shut, and then the truck's engine started. When Officer Meyer tried to talk to one of his teammates someone poked him in the ribs with a pointy object. He remained quiet. They drove seemingly only about a hundred yards before the truck stopped. And there they remained, silent, motionless, for three whole hours. He spent the time preparing his protestation, if he was ever afforded a chance to make one.

When the door opened, he launched straight into it: "We're Americans! You can't treat us like this. President Pence is going to have tanks rolling right through your shitty country within two motherfucking hours if you don't release me and my men right now."

"You are in charge?" said a voice with a heavy Spanish accent.

"Damn right I'm in charge."

Someone lifted the hood. The light was blinding. Unable to shield his eyes, he kept them closed at first. When he was able to open them a little he saw the man was wearing a sombrero and had a huge handlebar mustache.

"You will be released," the man said. "We're at the border now. Even though you attacked our country and shot up a motel room— you are absolutely right: Mexico doesn't want a war with the United States." The man smiled. "You are rich and all powerful, and we are merely poor and humble."

"Damn right," Officer Meyer said smugly. "What about our fugitive?"

"Señor Joseph Kaline is dead," the man said. "You shot him up quite nicely."

"What about our guns?" Officer Meyer asked.

"God knows we do not need more U.S. guns in Mexico. You can have your guns back once you are safely across the border. Your vehicles, however, we are confiscating until your government pays for the damage you did to El Motel Soñoliento del Gallo."

At that, Officer Meyer and his men were unbound and ushered to the pedestrian walkway of the Del Río-Ciudad Acuña International Bridge. Past the checkpoint, the man with the sombrero nodded and their guns were returned to them. As he led the procession across the bridge, Officer Meyer peeked in the HK's chamber: empty. The spics stole their ammunition.

Well, at least he had killed that Joseph Fucking Kaline—shot him so full of holes they'd probably have to bury him in a plastic bag.

Up ahead a handful of citizens of Del Río, having learned about the ALT Task Force's brave incursion into Mexico to pursue a terrorist, now stood waiting on the other side, waving an American flag and a banner that read "True American Heros!"

"Heroes" was misspelled, but this did nothing to diminish Officer Meyer's pride, which swelled his chest and his head. Yes, he was an American hero. A decade of arresting petty drug dealers in D.C. was nothing compared to this. As he beamed at the small crowd and declined to comment to the solitary news crew (fake news, anyway), he imagined getting summoned to the White House—President Mike Pence draping a medal around his neck.

Wouldn't that be something?

Getting a medal for something he wanted to do anyway: Make America Great Again!

Epilogue: The New Beginning

"My attorney advised me to not talk about politics..." The microphone squealed: looped signal. Clare cleared her throat, waited for the squeaking to stop, and gazed out at the audience. Hundreds had gathered: personal friends and family of the late Beach Sands; Super Court colleagues; admirers of the Fearless Vampire Killers—not by name, certainly—but by deed; journalists; and a handful of undercover cops. Seated in the front row, shrouded in black, Clare's attorney, Sarah Almeida, met her eyes and nodded approvingly. Clare continued: "But as Beach so often said, 'Fuck the World.'"

The crowd laughed, even Sarah—although she next narrowed her eyes and tilted her head, as if to warn: "Be careful, Clare. They're listening."

Reporters jotted in notebooks. Their cameramen crouching in the front corners snapped photos. Undercover agents adjusted the pinhole video cameras on their lapels. Beach's elderly parents, seated beside Sarah, held hands and quivered.

Clare clutched her gravid belly, only five months pregnant but nearly as big as a soccer ball on her petite frame. "Really, fuck the world. Fuck the world! Beach would be the first to admit that he wasn't a perfect man. He was judgmental and self-destructive. Had they not shot him down—an 'accidental discharge'—wink, wink—had that not happened—had they not *murdered* him, he may have been dead by now anyway. His death was slow—but painless—I've been told..." Here, her voice broke, tears streamed down her cheeks, and a sob escaped from her throat.

It was now easy to pick out the cops in the auditorium of the Josephine Butler Parks Center, the site of Beach's memorial service: they were the only ones whose eyes were still dry.

Clare composed herself and cleared her throat again. "Until today, I wasn't allowed to see or communicate with him. Did you know that? It was because, according to the indictment, we were both among the alleged 'conspirators, both known and unknown.' He never woke from his coma, so maybe it was just as well... The last time I saw him we were in the desert, and he was bleeding in my arms. You want to know the last thing he said to me?" She paused here for dramatic effect, sticking her tongue through the gap where her lateral incisor had once been. "He said—'Run.' They had just shot him, and that was his last word...

"But I didn't run. No, Beach—I didn't run. I refused to run. They threw me in jail. They charged me with Seditious Conspiracy, Terrorism, fucking *Treason*—and a lot of other crimes. My attorney—otherwise a brilliant lawyer—recommended I waive my right to a speedy trial. I refused. I'm sorry Sarah—but I'm not sorry. There are times in this world when something is so obviously wrong, so blatantly fucked up, that running from it or delaying the inevitable confrontation just perpetuates the injustice."

Cameras clicked. The reporters and cops perked up, waiting for Clare to say something—respectively—newsworthy or incriminating. In the front row, Sarah planted her face in her palm.

Clare took a sip of water, smiled. "The Treason charge was the kicker—a capital crime—and, as we all know, the President himself took a keen interest in my case. He ordered his prosecutors to pursue the death penalty against me—the fucking death penalty! Can you believe that? Again, my attorney—I think I'm going to give her a heart attack here today..." There was some nervous laughter. "Sarah urged me to plea bargain with them, to admit guilt and try to save my life. But again, there are times when running, delaying, bargaining— when those options just don't cut it. You can't bargain with sociopaths, because they're not honorable. They'll never—ever—live up to their part of the bargain. I know this.

"But as it turned out, for all the publicity my case generated and for all the legal handwringing, the government actually didn't have any evidence against me. Because of their 'accidental discharge,' Beach was incompetent to stand trial. Sure, they had some stuff on that Joseph Kaline character—his DNA or whatever—but they *murdered* him too. And so last week—after a hundred days in jail— following a three-week trial—after only deliberating six hours—the jury came back with a 'not guilty' on all counts."

The auditorium erupted in cheers. Again, the cops were conspicuous in their silence.

Once the applause died down, a reporter shouted, "Do you care to comment about the fourth 'unknown' conspirator?"

"This is a memorial service, not a press conference, so I do not care to comment about that." She took another sip of water. "When my verdict was announced, most of the country cheered—like what we just heard here—and they were right to celebrate." Hands again came together. The ovation lasted for a full minute. One cop slipped a hand inside his jacket, just to make sure the gun was still there. Clare waited until it grew quiet again. "But about a third of the country whined that it was just 'liberal jury nullification'—and maybe they're right too…"

"Are you concerned about state charges?" asked the same reporter.

Sarah Almeida turned and glowered at the man. "Ms. Swan is not taking questions now—so stop asking."

"When faced with evil—don't run, don't delay, and don't try to bargain with it." Clare smiled at Sarah, who shook her head nervously. "To be clear," she continued, "I'm not endorsing violence. I'm endorsing Beach's epitaph: fuck the world! Resist! Fuck the consequences! Fuck whomever you want! Fuck nationalism! Fuck jingoism! Fuck all -isms! Up with *people*! Empathy! Compassion! Sanity! Love!" Everyone but the cops stood. The obnoxious reporter was drowned out completely by the thunderous applause. "Beach Sands, for all his faults, was a good man, and I was a better person for knowing him. The world was better when he was around. I loved him, and I will miss him dearly. Thank you."

She wiped her eyes, waddled off the stage, hugged Beach's parents, Sarah, others—and then retreated down the stairs, ignoring the reporters and photographers. Others were preparing to give their eulogies, but Clare needed some fresh air. She left the Josephine Butler Center and crossed 15th Street to the Meridian Hill Park, more commonly known among Washingtonians as "Malcolm X Park." There she sat on a bench on the upper level overlooking the fountain, dabbing her eyes and thinking about Beach and Joe. She touched her belly—her baby. Was it Beach's, Joe's, or FD's? She had no idea. She needed to be more careful. She feared she had said too much at the eulogy. The Commonwealth of Virginia was weighing state charges, as were a few other jurisdictions. Anything she said might be used against her.

Upon these thoughts a woman, short, skin like red clay, red dot on her forehead, approached the bench. "Your words were very moving."

"Thank you."

"I am Geeta—Joe's wife." Clare's mouth dropped open, stayed there, and before she could respond Geeta opened her hand and said, "There is someone here to see you."

From behind a tree stepped a massive figure, skin like polished walnut—but with short hair—lumpy head malformed, beautiful. He flashed a crooked smile.

"Holy shit!" Clare leapt from the bench and threw her arms around FD. She touched his head. "You look completely different! I hardly recognize you."

He glanced at her round belly, smirked, then turned and presented a woman who had been standing behind him. "This is my partner, Azul."

Azul had skin like amber and black hair held back with a headband—three feathers poking out the back. "It's nice to meet you, Clare." They shook hands politely.

FD, Geeta, and Azul then turned toward the fountain, and there he was: Joe Kaline—alive—sitting at a picnic table inside an enclave, beside a young boy wearing shorts, tussled black hair, skin like café au lait.

Clare scanned the park to make sure they were alone, and then ran to Joe and the boy. "But how… They said you were dead!" She wrapped her arms around him.

He put a hand on her belly, smirked. "The Mexican police lied to the U.S. government. They hate President Pence so much they'll do anything to burn him. They even gave me a Mexican passport. I'm now 'Harry Vasquez.'"

She laughed. "Do you even speak Spanish?"

"No, I didn't stay in Mexico long. I flew to India after a month."

She turned to FD. "But how did you two find each other?"

"Remember, I used to be a private detective," Joe said. "I searched the country for Ef-dee's art. I know his style. I found him living in Albuquerque."

"I got a gig painting murals there," FD said. "Last week Joe just showed up and said we should come watch the end of your trial. Then we learned Beach died…"

Harry Vasquez, once known as Joseph Kaline and even Joseph *Fucking* Kaline, also Jack—and perhaps other names, now forgotten—looked around and folded the conspirators, which now included Geeta and Azul, into his arms. Standing near the fountain, they resembled a football huddle. Naagesh, curious, stood nearby.

Harry said, "I came back because Geeta's uncle was one of the designers on the National Trump Memorial in New Jersey. He can get us inside before the unveiling ceremony next week. Can you imagine what Ef-dee could do to that monument if we could just get him alone in there for a couple days?"

Clare clutched her belly. "I don't know. Things have changed a lot in the last five months. I'm going to be a mom. I know what I said at Beach's memorial, but I'd prefer *not* to live the rest of my life in a prison."

"There's no chance of that," Geeta said. "My uncle won't even know he helped us. He doesn't even know that we're in the U.S. right now."

Clare's eyes turned to Naagesh, who smiled back at her innocently. "I'm *not* agreeing to your plan, but I don't suppose there's any harm in us just talking about it—wishfully speaking, of course."

"Sure, wishing ain't illegal—not yet."

About the Author

Philip Becnel has managed a private detective business in Washington, D.C. for nearly twenty years. "Freedom City" is his debut novel, but he previously published two nonfiction books: "Introduction to Conducting Private Investigations" and "Principles of Investigative Documentation."

He lives in D.C. with a magnificent partner and has two precocious teenagers. When he's not writing or investigating, he loves to paint, backpack, fight with swords, and travel to far-flung places.

Despite what this book may imply, he despises politics.